Creative Writing Stories

A Collection of Short Stories Written by Members of the Atria Willow Glen Creative Writing Group

Foreword

The Atria Willow Glen Creative Writing Group meets bi-weekly, with members writing short stories which are shared with the other members at each meeting. To help stimulate the members to write a variety of new stories, the leader often passes out short clips, known as writing prompts, in advance of each meeting, to form the basis for their submissions.

Since its inception the group has published five different books containing short stories. This sixth book, *Creative Writing Stories*, contains stories which the members felt represented some of the best of their 2018 works. By collecting them in this book, they are able to share them with you.

Elvet Moore
Resident Instructor
Creative Writing Group

Table of Contents

Table of Contents

(Continued)

Table of Contents
(Concluded)

Chuck Northup

Betty Stearns

Betty Wyatt

Family Quarry

Atria: Who Am I?

By Bonnie Bliss

I arrive like a new book—my pages are all blank.
My life is secret and hidden until I share.
Everything is revealed—one conversation at a time.
A shadow arrived—and slowly my past is revealed.

I move through my new life—adding and subtracting stories.
I'm anxious to sparkle—and to share the joy of my life.
I'm reluctant to outshine my current companions.
I fight to reclaim my whole self—to seek relevance.

My present is limited—will I allow it to define me?
Will my whole life be relevant in this new prescribed one?
Will my life be reduced to a single story?
Will my whole life be a part of who I am today?

Or is my life reduced to the story of a good book?
Will all of my past combine to transform into my present?

Ghost of the Black Bear
By Bonnie Bliss

Reuben heard the whisper when he entered San Francisco Bay in 1848. The voice was telling him to come see the elephant—to join the miners searching for gold in California.

The voice said to Reuben, "Come look for gold."

So Reuben jumped ship and headed to Sonora to pan for gold. He first saw the Black Bear fishing at the river. Reuben heard the voice again and realized that the bear was talking to him.

The Black Bear said to Reuben, "Come look for gold in the Trinity Alps."

Reuben bought a mule and followed the other miners—hiking the 49er trail to Yreka and to the Salmon River mines.

With sun in his eyes, Reuben saw the ghost of the Black Bear again. "Come look for gold on the North Fork of the Salmon River."

3

So Reuben and his mule climbed over the mountain and down into the Salmon River Valley.

The ghost of the Black Bear said to Reuben, "Come look for gold further up the river."

Reuben turned up the North Fork and panned along the river. The Black Bear was right. There was gold to be found in the river.

The ghost of the Black Bear said to Reuben, "Come look for gold at the Black Bear Gulch."

The Black Bear was at the river fishing when he first talked to Reuben. The bear stood and rambled up the gulch. Reuben knew that he should follow.

The ghost of the Black Bear said to Reuben, "Come, climb that hill and look for a quartz outcropping."

Much to Reuben's surprise he found quartz spilling out from the hill.

The ghost of the Black Bear said to Reuben, "Come, dig here."

With his pick-ax Reuben started to chip at the quartz. And there was gold there—lots of gold.

The Black Bear and Reuben shouted, "Eureka, we have found it."

The ghost of the Black Bear whispered to Reuben, "You should file a claim for this gold mine."

Reuben went into town with his bag of gold nuggets. He filed his Black Bear Mine claim. He bought a lumber mill and a carpenter shop. He needed the logs to shore up the falling rocks in his mine tunnels. He bought a water flume, too. The mine needed more water to flush the gold rocker boxes.

Reuben and his ghost returned to the mine. The Black Bear said, "The mine is doing well—you should now invest in property."

They continued to have luck finding gold. On his next trip to town Reuben bought three lots in the town of Trinidad. Reuben could see that the same lode continued up the hill, so he traded shares of his mine for a partnership in the next mine. That is the way the miners did business. If the mine needed water Reuben traded for shares in the water flume—if the mine needed more logs, Reuben traded for shares in the lumber mill. Soon the Black Bear mine had many partners.

The Black Bear told Reuben, "Register all of the mines and the new partners."

When the Black Bear, the Yellow Jacket, the Sawyers Bar, and the Hard Scrabble mines were all combined, and the lumber mills and the water flumes were all combined—there were 38 partners altogether. Again the partners went to town to register the new business and record their various shares.

The mines needed to grow—The Black Bear told Reuben and his partners, "Invest in stamp mills."

Stamp mills were purchased and transported to Sawyers Bar to help crush the gold ore. Bringing in the stamp mills was very difficult. The mules could each carry only a small load, so a train of mules was needed to traverse the narrow winding mountain trail to Sawyers Bar.

The trip was made safely and the new mills increased production greatly. The stamp mills were very dangerous and one of the first casualties was Reuben. His arm was caught in the stamp mill and he died the same day of hemorrhage.

The ghost of the Black Bear had been a good friend to Reuben. With his help and good luck the family prospered in the gold fields. Reuben said "good-bye" to the Black Bear.

Notes: Reuben and his brother Charles had been partners in the Black Bear Mine since they had arrived in Trinidad. Reuben's brother, Charles, was still in the area—he lived and worked in Trinidad Town. Trinidad was an important harbor for whaling. The ships would unload the barrels of rendered whale oil for storage on land awaiting the ships' return to the east.

Charles owned several town lots and held the mortgage on several others, but his big project was building the Trinidad Wharf. With the permission of the California State Legislature, he used his carpentry skills to construct a wharf in the Bay. He carved a ledge just above the high water level on Trinidad Head, the largest island in Trinidad Bay. He constructed a wharf attached to the rock and built a floating dock for the ships. The harbor was a convenient port close to the Trinity mining district. The wharf allowed ships to anchor and unload their cargo and move it onto shore.

Charles lived and whaled from his uncle's ship based in Trinidad. When the whaling ship returned to Massachusetts, Charles was on board. He brought a small pouch of gold back to his mother in Yarmouth,

Nova Scotia. He traveled with a mining friend, Michael Macraith, who was from New York. Charles met Ellen on this trip; (Michael's sister). She became his future wife.

Ellen followed Charles and her brother, Michael, to California within two years with her own trip across Panama. Charles and Ellen married in San Francisco and then moved to Trinidad and Sawyers Bar to be near the mines. With Reuben's passing, Charles was left to take over the mine.

There were many miners in the area now, and the local Indians were starting to bother the miners. The miners had moved onto Indian land—the Indians were displaced and starving. The Indians stole the miner's cattle and the miners fought back. Ellen fell pregnant amid this chaos, and chose to return to San Francisco for the birth. She left on a mule with Charles following a few months later. The mine shares were sold—the houses and the other interests were also sold. Charles bought a coal and feed business in San Francisco.

They Met Skating

By Bonnie Bliss

A cousin told me, "They met roller skating." Using my research skills and documents on hand, I would like to recreate the story of my grandparents.

William Patrick Jennings was born in San Francisco on 19 July 1889. He was the fourth of eleven children—the oldest boy. When his father, Patrick, died in a steamboat explosion near Rio Vista in 1902, he was left as the bread winner for the family. He dropped out of school and found a job in the mailroom of the Southern Pacific Railroad. The headquarters was just a few blocks from his home on Jessie Street.

After Patrick's death, Margaret, Patrick's widow, moved the Jennings family from Jessie Street in downtown San Francisco to her parents' small farm on Third Street in San Mateo. I have been told that the property backed onto the San Mateo Creek and that there were ducks guarding the driveway. Margaret, my great grandmother on that side, remarried Max Broska. He is listed in census records as a seaman. The family called them Grandpa and Grandma Max.

Grand-daddy-boy continued to live in San Francisco and work for Southern Pacific. He was forced to retire at age 60, just a few years before being associated with the Southern Pacific for 50 years. In 1912, when William Patrick Jennings and Martha Heins met, he was moving up in the Southern Pacific Company. He had returned to school and graduated from Business College. Grand-daddy-boy described his years at Southern Pacific as starting in the basement in the mailroom at age 13—moving to jobs in accounting on the middle floors,—and then moving to his retirement in administration on the top floor.

Martha Louise Heins was the youngest of three children. She was born in New York on 23 July 1889 to German immigrant parents. Luis Heins, her father, was a go-getter who ran a saloon at 18th and Diamond in San Francisco. Nana was a beautiful strawberry blond. Pictures from that time show that she was a very smart, fashionable dresser. I have pictures of them on their wedding day. The first is a formal photo with them both standing at attention facing each other smiling at the camera. The second is of them horsing around. It looks like Grand-daddy-boy was trying to pull Nana's hair or maybe he was trying to steal a kiss. It was a double exposure that I have cleaned up a bit with photo shop.

Checking a directory of San Francisco for the year 1912, the Fillmore district is shown to have a skating rink. Grand-daddy-boy was a young working Irish man and Nana was a beautiful German girl. This is where I would expect that my grandparents met.

Grand-daddy-boy played baseball for a semi-pro team for a few years, but when I knew him his sports interest was in watching Billy (his son) play football for Poly High in San Francisco.

Nana loved her family. Her mother, Bertha Heins, lived with them for years after she was widowed. She shared a bedroom with her grand-daughters. Nana took care of her invalid mother for many years after Bertha's stroke.

Nana had four married children and eleven grandchildren—she therefore had a birthday or holiday party several times a month. She loved to cook and to celebrate with her family. During WWII Nana's younger married daughters lived at home while their husbands served in the war. During the summer Nana had the Sonoma house filled with grand-kids. Grand-daddy-boy and the children came up on weekends, but the grandkids stayed all summer.

Billy was the star quarterback of the Poly High football team. The Call Bulletin paper had the headline that year asking, "Can Billy come out to play?" He went to the University of San Francisco on a football scholarship, he was a lifelong 49'ers fan, and he volunteered as usher for most home games.

Grandpa Judge

By Bonnie Bliss

William Boniface Ryder, senior, was born in 1868, married in 1905, and died in 1947. He was alive for the first ten years of my life, yet I have no vivid memories of him. My memories are based on family stories and photos.

The front room at Nana Ryders house was always dark with the curtains drawn so no outside light ever crept in. Grandpa Judge had his big overstuffed chair in the darkest corner of the room. A cloud of cigar smoke hovered around his chair. The only movement was the glow of the cigar as he moved it to his mouth. When we entered the house we were warned, "Keep your voices down—or you will disturb Grandpa Judge."

Grandpa Judge was born and raised in the Mission District of San Francisco. In 1874, Charles, his father, died and Ellen, his mother, was left with five small children. Ellen remarried within a year to a policeman friend of her brother, Michael. John Marsh and the three older boys ran the coal and hay business for a year or so—but John's death saw the family moving to Alameda Island.

Recent visits to Alameda suggest that Grandpa Judge and his brothers had marshes and beaches to explore—for the US Naval Air Station was not built until 1927.

Two of the boys were sent to a school near Santa Barbara, where the air was considered better for their hay fever. The sisters stayed in San Francisco, and one supported herself by giving piano and art lessons. She later became a nun, Sister Mary Gonzaga. The other sister married a dentist and lived in San Diego with her family.

The family lore of gold mining must have been enticing, since all three of the sons went to the mines—first to Nevada City on the Yuba River, and then further afield. One died immediately after his return from his mine in Ransburg, while another mined in Carson City, Nevada, for many years.

Grandpa Judge spent twenty years or more in the mines of California and Nevada. My grandfather's last mining adventure was in Tonopah, Nevada. His silver mine was located in the flat desert outside of town (not very profitable). When I visited in the 1990s there was only about three feet of wooden fencing left to mark the opening to the mine tunnels.

My one day of research in Tonopah was not very fruitful. I was just getting into the records when they closed the office for a two-hour lunch break. I was tossed out of the hot court house into the sunny 110 degree noon-day sun. I drove to the mine, then back to Ridgecrest to my daughter Shannon's house. I planned another trip sometime in the winter, but never got around to it.

Grandpa Judge was forty years old when he returned from the mines, and he found an 18-year-old Irish girl to wed. They married and started a family soon thereafter.

Grandpa Judge worked at Hibernia Bank as a clerk for several years before he read for the Bar. In 1913 he began calling himself an attorney in the city directory. His glory days were the years he worked with the Tobin brothers building Hibernia Bank's resources

15

and reputation. He was the attorney for Hibernia bank until the end of his life. He had an office at the bank that he visited a few hours a week, but he was long retired from active law during my years.

In all my research I have never found evidence that Grandpa Judge was ever a judge. Documents I found in the Tonopah City Hall records office show that William B. (Boniface) Ryder served as Justice of the Peace for the town. Perhaps this is the origin of his 'Grandpa Judge' name.

My memories of my grandfather are found in the pictures from Daddy's family. The first picture I remember is of a group of smartly dressed young people hiking in the mountains above Mineral King in the Sierras. Dad had a maternal grandmother and cousins in Visalia and Exeter in the central valley of California. The picture shows the group sitting atop a mountain overlooking the valley with more mountains in the distance. My grandfather is dressed in his three-piece business suit, white shirt and vest buttoned up, wearing a tie. He is posed standing on top of a rock, with his ever present cigar in his hand. He was ready to conquer the world, or at least that mountain.

I recently looked again at the photo and I can see that one of the women, dressed in a corseted fashionable dress, is my grandmother. She had no cigar, but she did have a smart hat and fine shoes. Imagine hiking in the Sierras in a corset and high button shoes.

Another photo of that time is of a group of young men standing around a new car. The story I remember is that Grandpa Judge drove his new car to show it off to his cousins in Exeter. Grandpa Judge is standing proudly by the driver's door—again dressed in a suit, vest and tie—holding his ever present cigar.

The third photo is of the family group sitting in the shade of the San Francisco house. Nana Ryder is in a chair—the baby buggy is beside her, and Grandpa Judge is standing, holding my father still dressed in his baptismal gown. Again Grandpa Judge is smoking his cigar.

The story Dad told every Sunday at dinner was of his Sundays as a boy. The family would be up early. Nana Ryder and Alice, dad's sister, would dress and go to church. Dad and his father would head for the Ferry Building and take the ferry to Marin. From there by train to Mill Valley and then they would climb

Mount Tamalpais—most Sundays to the top. After a rest they would head for home. By mid-afternoon the family would be around the big dining room table for a leg of lamb, roasted potatoes, and mixed vegetables.

The bit I remember vividly was the table set using silver, crystal and good china. Each place had a silver napkin ring holding a crisp linen napkin. Grandpa Judge would stand at the table head and carve the roast, Nana Ryder was sitting at her end, and she would serve the side dishes. Between them around the table would be the whole family. After dinner the men would retire to the living room for drinks and of course, Grandpa's cigar.

The meal was formal with the tablecloth that Nana Ryder had crocheted, along with silver and the O'Hare china, etc. Grandpa Judge would carve the roast from the head of the table, while we all watched. The O'Hare siblings of Nana Ryder lived with them until they had homes and wives of their own. They would be at the table, also.

The side board had a huge silver punch bowl and twelve cups on a giant silver tray. An extraordinary eighteen inch butter dish was there too. It featured a six inch globe, the top half of which would slide up the handles to sit hovering above the butter inside the globe. This family treasure was stolen in the 2016 robbery, but it is shown in the pictures of BonBon's Mothers Day dinner that year.

As the oldest grandchildren on both sides of our families, Bill and I both inherited family treasures. With my girls both living from home, I no longer cooked big family dinners. With Bill being gone for over ten years I was moaning about the fact that my grandchildren would never see a big family dinner using all of the inherited dinner service.

So, for Mother's Day in 2016, the girls surprised me with a formal dinner. I set the table for my grandchildren, explaining the history of each piece as we set the table.

The lace tablecloth was crocheted by Nana Ryder. The Reindeer napkins were brought from Germany by Bertha Cappelmann Heins. Silver napkin rings were from Ryder. The crystal water, wine, and champagne glasses were from the Bliss & Baumgarten families. The china was my wedding set. The gold rimed place plates were inherited from Alice Bliss. The dessert was served in the crystal bowls from Alice's collection. The silver pepper shakers were Bliss. The salt dishes and tiny silver spoons were Ryder. The carving set with Elk Horn handles were Bliss. The serving spoons were Bliss, Ryder, and Jennings. The crystal water pitcher was Bliss.

Pacific Paradise

By Bonnie Bliss

The wedding was beautiful—the old Ross Church glowed with the sun streaming through the stained glass windows. The church was crowded—the groom's mother insisted the church held 500 people, not the 300 the minister told us.

The reception was a 30-minute drive into the hills at the Meadow Club. The green golf course was quiet and served as a serene backdrop for the pictures. Inside all went as scheduled. The bridesmaids in pink sheaths with lace bolero jackets carried pink carnation leis for the ceremony and wore them Hawaiian style at the reception.

The bride and groom changed and climbed into the Alpha Romero Speedster with the top down, to fly down the hill to be alone at last. In the back were the suitcases, along with midnight snack boxes packed by the caterer. There were also three wedding cake boxes we were scheduled to deliver to family and friends who missed the wedding.

First was Bill's Aunt Libs' box. She would be easy—she lived across from the Marina Green barely off the Golden Gate Bridge. Since we married on a Saturday and it was now mid-afternoon, we drove around and around the block looking for parking but there were yacht races on the bay that day. Parking wasn't easy as one wrong turn put us back on the bridge on our way back to Marin. However, on the third lap past Lib's house we found parking about two blocks away.

Dressed smartly in my camel going away suit with lizard heels and handbag, we walked two blocks and climbed three flights of stairs, to be greeted and welcomed inside. We delivered the cake and told our wedding story. I limped back to the car on my three inch pointy-toed heels, over two hours later.

Second were Bill's Aunt Olivine and Uncle Bill, surrogate grandparents to Bill. Their home was out near the beach in West Portal, where they had prepared a small snack for our visit. The visit was rushed but did take about three hours. After that we were on our way again.

Our last stop was to my grandmother—she had been in a nursing home for over a year recovering from a stroke. After she had her cake and heard all about our big day she marched us door to door to show us off. We got to hear everyone's medical history along the way.

It was dark now, about six hours after leaving the reception, and we were still in San Francisco, but that was the last stop! We had planned an early dinner but decided we really weren't hungry yet. So we drove south toward Palo Alto, our first night's destination.

Remember, this was 1964, and the highways weren't built yet. El Camino Real seemed to be a smart route choice from the beach. The Alpha roadster was warmer now with the top up, but the wind and fog managed to slip in.

We looked for a decent restaurant, but all were closed. El Camino had stop lights at every block and a 25-30 mile per hour speed limit. We inched our way to Palo Alto and our first nights' accommodations at Ricky's Cabana Resort Hotel.

We got there about mid-night—cold, tired, and hungry. Bill left me in the car while he registered. Our room was not in the regular part of the hotel but in an outside wing around back.

What a room it was! The room was dominated by the biggest bed I had ever seen. One wall had a big dresser with a mirror along the wall behind it. Another wall had mirrored closet doors, floor to ceiling, and wall to wall. We didn't notice the mirror over the bed until we were in bed.

There was lots of car traffic—cars coming and going, slamming doors, cranking motors, and gunning engines all night. We were the only guests to stay all night. Our suppositions were right. We had spent our wedding night in the red light wing of the Cabana Hotel.

The next day after brunch, we started for Palm Springs. Our first stop however was at Bill's parents' home. Since Bill was just back from Kodiak, we needed details of our reservations waiting in Palm Springs. We embarked on a day of driving through California's Central Valley—then on into the desert.

The flaw in the plan was that we didn't have a map in the car, so Bill was choosing routes randomly as we wound our way along. I was hot, tired, and a bit carsick from the new birth control pills—big weddings are big stress makers. I wanted a swim, and a nap. Bill on the other hand just wanted to drive and drive, to race along the country roads in the desert— leaving to chance if we ever found Palm Springs. I eventually faked a need for a potty-break and while inside I bought a map. I was right—we were heading away from Palm Springs.

Our motel had been selected by Bill's parents and their friends as the cheapest motel in Palm Springs. It was cheap because it was miles from town. There were no restaurants for miles and the vending machines were empty. Never let your parents make your honeymoon arrangements.

Well, it was our first honeymoon, so we did have a quiet loving time. Eventually it was time to go home to sort out all of our worldly goods into three groups—items Alaska bound, items for storage at Blisses,' and items for storage at Ryder's.

Alaska bound items contained a minimum of household goods, all of my city shoes, and my party dresses, three suitcases and two trunks in all. Bliss storage items had Bill's science fiction book collection, the three generations of crystal wine, water, and champagne glasses, and a few other wedding gifts left with Bill's folks. The Ryder family had the rest of the wedding presents, the bulk of my wardrobe, and some family treasures of mine.

Finally, we were away after a big good-bye at the airport. We were on our way to our Pacific Island Paradise, Kodiak, Alaska.

x x x

27 March, 1964: Alaska experienced a 9.2 level earthquake and devastating tsunami . . .

Just Before Santa Arrives

By Bonnie Bliss

I am awake early and the house is quiet. I sneak into the living room. It's dark, lit only by the street light outside the front window. The Xmas tree is silhouetted against the dark night.

Hanging from the mantle are four stockings. Dad's has a can of Almond Roca Chocolates sticking out the top. Mom says every year, "Bill is so hard to shop for. Santa always brings him chocolates."

The children's stockings are filled (by family tradition) with pens, pencils, erasers, tooth brushes, tooth paste, ribbons, and hair bows, but way down in the toe each girl will find a birthstone ring or necklace.

Under the tooth brushes, curlers, and lip balm, Mom's stocking is filled with lottery tickets. After all, she did the stocking stuffer shopping for all of us.

A quick check under the tree shows piles of books, and a few toys. Santa always brings stacks of presents to our house, but inside are only practical gifts—new PJs, underwear, socks, robe, and slippers, for example.

There will be one new outfit to wear to the family Xmas dinner. I helped shop for mine. I know I will get a plaid skirt with matching pullover and cardigan sweaters—green this year, since that is my current favorite color.

Gifts from Dad are always unwrapped and unusual. This year he shopped at the drug store. There are three big plastic boxes filled with hair stuff, curlers, rollers, bobby pins, wave clips, a new brush, a comb and some hair spray. The note from Dad reminds us that there will be no more fights, as we each will have our own hair stuff now.

The bridal doll I had been asking Santa for was not there again this year. I will probably be a teenager before I have a beautiful bridal doll to display on my bed. Gloria, my best friend has one on her bed, and it looks so elegant. I wanted one, too.

I check out the faint ticking I hear from the back of the tree. There is a rather large box that I know is for my grandmother. Mom found an antique clock for her—she can put it on her fireplace mantel.

It is still early, and no one else is up, so after I have un-wrapped and wrapped all of my gifts, I go back to bed. An hour or so later I hear Dagmar, our dog, barking at the back door to get out. Soon thereafter, I hear her dog claws tap along the hall to my room. Now it is time for everyone to get up.

Merry Christmas to all!

Bear Hunt

By Bonnie Bliss

I walked silently through the forest. I have a client next week—a game hunter, hoping to bag some Kodiak bears. He is determined—he plans to stay for a week or so tracking for his kill. I have contacts at Kodiak Fish and Game, and they have spotted and counted several bears on the island, so I know how many kills are possible this summer.

My job today is to find the bears, note their territories, and plan for a week-long hunt. With luck and careful planning, we can have several sightings during the week, but no kill will be made until the last day. My hunter pays me by the day and he has deep pockets, so I plan a nice long week of tracking.

Walking upstream, I am aware that the creek is in full spawn. The water is teaming with salmon fighting their way to the breeding pools further inland. I haven't spotted scat or bear tracks yet. The weather is just changing to warm days, and there are still pockets of snow in shady spots. The bear should be fishing soon.

As I round the bend of the creek trail I spot a Kodiak female. She spots me at the same time, so she rears up ready to attack. She is still lean from her winter hibernation, but when she stands erect she towers over me and the undergrowth.

Something is wrong. She should be hungry and more interested in the salmon than in me. Quickly, I glance around. Oh, God, I am between her and her cubs. Immediately I drop into a passive position. I curl into a ball for protection—my arms covering my face and eyes, and my legs are drawn up to protect my abdomen.

She continues to advance, running toward me at full speed with her claws spread to attack. I roll toward a tree curling into it for added protection—lying deadly still. She attacks first with unsheathed claws. She rakes my back and head trying to disable me quickly.

She probes and malls me to uncover my eyes and abdomen. I hang on protecting myself. She is roaring

32

and growling. I am biting my tongue to remain silent and still. She prods and tosses me around until she determines that I am dead.

Convinced that I am dead she collects her cubs and ambles off into the forest toward the creek. I lay lifeless in the dirt and leaves, mentally taking inventory of my injuries. No bones are broken, my eyes are intact, but there are deep painful scratches on my back, arms, and legs. I have scratches to the bone on one elbow.

I must get away. I radio my SOS and position to the Fish and Game. They arrange for a helicopter to pick me up and airlift me to the local hospital. I wrap my arms and legs to stop the bleeding while I wait. I anticipate two months in the hospital to heal and fight infection. There will not be much of a hunting season this year for me.

Rabbit's Honey

By Tom Brandt (with apologies to A.A. Milne)

Once upon a time, a five-year-old lad named Christopher Robin lived with his parents in the English countryside. He owned a menagerie of anthropomorphized stuffed animals. The grounds around his house contained, among other delights, a grove of fir trees.

Amongst the numerous fir trees there was raised an occasional English oak that had somehow escaped the axes of the Royal Navy. In the eyes of a five-year-old, this was certainly a hundred acres of woods, and Christopher Robin's menagerie had residences scattered through this hundred-acre wood.

Christopher Robin's stuffed teddy bear, named Edward, held the prize position among the animals. Edward Bear had a prodigious appetite for honey. He frequently had a ring of honey around his muzzle which tended to attract flies. He would puff them away with a sound like "poof". In the fullness of time, he became known as Pooh Bear and finally simply Pooh.

One fine spring day Pooh took his afternoon constitutional through the Hundred-Acre Wood. As the afternoon wore on, Pooh began to feel like he needed a little something in his tummy. Teatime approached as he came near to Rabbit's warren. He paused.

"Hallo Rabbit," he called.

Rabbit's face appeared at the entrance to the rabbit hole. "Hallo Pooh." After a moment, she emerged through the guardian gorse bush and stood before Pooh.

In the awkward silence that followed, Pooh began to wonder if he had made a mistake, but Rabbit said, "I've just put the teakettle on. Won't you come in?"

Pooh said, "Delighted."

However, this was easier said than done. Pooh followed Rabbit through the gorse bush. The rabbit hole was made for lithe and supple rabbits and Pooh had grown rather stout. Pooh got down on his belly and from that position, he could reach neither his hands nor his knees. With a tug from Rabbit, he popped into Rabbit's living room.

He regained his feet, dusted himself off, and sat in one of Rabbit's easy chairs. Rabbit kept a small but tidy house. She laid the tea on a coffee table and set a pot of honey within reach.

The rest of the afternoon sped away as Pooh and Rabbit discussed the affairs of the Hundred-Acre Wood. Pooh reached for a honey pot, but Rabbit said, "Pooh, there isn't any more honey." Indeed, the coffee table now held four empty honey pots.

"I guess it's time for me to be on my way," said Pooh.

He rose and headed for the rabbit hole. He reached out his forepaws and grasped the sides of the hole. He pulled and managed to get about a third of the way through. He did get his head and arms outside. But then he got stuck fast.

"Oh bother."

Rabbit went out her back door and came around to the front and pulled hard. Pooh moved another few inches.

Rabbit sat down for a breath. After a brief pause, she said, "I'll get Christopher Robin. He'll know what to do," and scurried off.

Left to himself Pooh began to hum. "Isn't it funny how a bear likes honey?"

Tum tum tum I wonder why he does come?"

Presently, Christopher Robin came into view.

"Hallo Pooh. Got yourself in a tight spot, I see."

Pooh tried to grunt, but the rabbit hole squeezed his breath away.

The lad continued, "Give us a hand and we'll have you out in a jiffy."

He took Pooh's paws in his hands and leaned back.

"Ow!" said Pooh.

"That didn't work, did it?" said Christopher Robin. "Guess we'll have to send you back into the house."

He reversed his grip on Pooh's forepaws and shoved with all his strength.

"Ow!" and then, "Oh Bother," escaped from the Bear's lips.

"No better," said the boy. "You are well and truly stuck."

Christopher Robin stroked his head. "The only thing I can think of is for you to wait here until you've lost enough weight to get out. How does that sound?"

"Terrible," said the bear.

"Worse," said Rabbit. "I've got to use my back door for as long as Pooh's stuck here."

Christopher Robin thought for a moment and then said, "Tell you what. I'll get Nanny to come over here and read to us. How does that sound?"

"No better," said Pooh.

Nonetheless, no one came up with a better plan, so for the next four days, Pooh remained stuck fast in Rabbit's front door. Christopher Robin stopped by every day to chat with Pooh. Nanny came twice.

On the morning of the fourth day, Rabbit assembled an array of her friends and relations— seven rabbits, five hedgehogs, three voles, and an indeterminate number of mice—to join in a Great Tug.

Christopher Robin took Pooh's right paw and the assembly, led by the seven rabbits, took his left. Rabbit herself went inside the house to push from behind. Christopher Robin took charge and gave the word, "Ready, NOW!"

"Ow!" Pooh said as he flew from the hole, capsizing five of the seven rabbits into the thickest part of the gorse bush. Christopher Robin held fast to Pooh's right paw and set him upon his feet. Rabbit scampered out through her now open front door and scowled at the damage wrought to the gorse bush as well as the entrance hole itself. Christopher Robin busied himself helping the lead rabbits remove the gorse spines they acquired when Pooh dumped them into the bush.

Pooh dusted him off, looked around, and said, "I feel I need a little something in my tummy." He then set off in the direction of the hollow oak tree where he lived.

Christopher Robin was heard to mutter, "Silly old bear."

My Grandfathers

By Tom Brandt

My grandfathers were not part of my life. Grandfather Worthen died two years before I was born. Grandfather Brandt was widowed when my dad was four years old, and my grandmother's family swooped in to take care of the motherless lad. They took him from his home in Pinole to their place in Stockton.

The families became estranged, although I never knew why. Aunt Carrie and Uncle Walter took good care of my dad, leading to his graduation from Stanford in the class of 1926. Living in Ohio as my parents did made contact with the California relatives a virtual impossibility, especially during the depression years.

Both my parents were only children, so our nuclear family is all but non-existent. My best elder generation story, therefore, comes from my Great Uncle Riley who owned a dairy farm in upstate New York. Riley married Florence—the youngest sister of my grandmother. They lived near Adams Center which is about thirty miles south of Watertown. Grandmother's next youngest sister, spinster Grace, lived with their bachelor brother, James, in the Watertown family home. We visited Watertown and environs quite regularly during the prewar years. We may have gone every summer before gas rationing.

Riley was a colorful man. He had served in the marines and participated in one of our country's incursions into Nicaragua during the Gunboat Diplomacy era of the late nineteenth century. I've been told that he played in the band, but I never saw a musical instrument. It might have been a drum.

He had a vivid imagination which played well with a six-year-old grandnephew. He and I discovered a fabulous jungle that was full of tigers—in truth underneath the dining room table. I spent many happy hours hunting the fearsome felines, by crawling around among the legs of that great table. Remember that this was a farm dining room so there were many mouths to feed with the extended family of Riley and Florence, their son with his wife, and children plus the seasonal hired hands.

In adult retrospective, the table is not nearly as huge as I remembered and why it was such a satisfactory jungle escapes me now. As a born and bred city kid the farm was always a magical place for me. Even the last time we visited, shortly after the war was over and gas rationing had been lifted, I found mysteries and new discoveries for my then know-it-all high school mind to uncover.

Happiness is hunting tigers under the dining room table!

An Afternoon's Adventure

By Tom Brandt

Twas a fine mid-summer day when I set out for the convenience store on the corner. I was annoyed with myself for allowing the liquid hand soap to run out, but certainly the corner store would have at least a quart refill. I whistled softly as I walked along the block and a half to the store.

The Jenkins lived half a block from the store and their mutt stood guard at the fence line. It eyed me carefully as I walked past, but made no sound. Once in the store, I found the refills right away and stepped to the counter where the proprietor stood waiting.

"Hi George. Will that be all today?"

"Yeah. I'm so stupid to let this stuff run out on me."

"Not to worry. That's why I'm here. Ever play the lottery?"

45

"Nah. I'm not that stupid."

"The big prize is out of sight again. Why not start small. Buy yourself one scratch ticket. It's only a buck."

"Bill, I don't think so. Somehow those things never work for me."

"Oh, come on. Don't be such a chicken. Just one ticket."

"Oh, all right. Gimme one."

I took the ticket and duly scratched off the magic space.

"My God! It says here that I won fifty bucks. How can that be?"

"I told you to play. Here, give me the ticket." Bill went to the lottery safe to deposit the ticket and returned with a crisp fifty-dollar bill. "Want to play some more?"

"No way. Give me what I won. I'm going home to celebrate."

I turned to leave but hesitated. "No, give me a box of chocolates, too."

With my purchases safely in a bag, I left the store for the walk home. This time the Jenkins' dog greeted me with a robust serenade. The barking dog had somehow sensed that I carried food and followed me along the fence as far as the property allowed.

"Go away," I said. "Chocolate's not good for dogs, so you don't get any."

The dog persisted nearly the entire block. I had to cross the street before the beast conceded. A FedEx truck pulled away from the curb very near my house.

"That's odd. We don't get many of them in this neighborhood."

As I neared the house, I realized that there was now a package on my front stoop. I wasn't expecting anything so I approached the box with gentle steps. I heard a soft ticking sound from inside. My heart skipped a beat and then began to race. Images of shredded people from bomb attacks ran through my mind.

I pulled out my cell phone. The 911 operator was patient with me as I breathlessly tried to describe my ticking package. While I was talking with her, the sounds changed to a soft whirring that generated two short chimes followed by a single chime. The ticking continued.

The operator kept me on the line until the first wave of cops had arrived and taken command of the situation. I was pushed aside to allow for the area to be taped and cleared. As they worked, the significance of the chimes slowly sunk into my distracted mind. I looked at my watch. One forty-seven in the afternoon. So that's it. By then more cops had arrived and busied themselves with securing the area. I tried to slow their progress but got dismissed as a busybody neighbor.

I found a sergeant and started to explain my situation. The box chimed again, this time two strokes followed by two more—two o'clock—right on time.

"Officer, stop! I know what's inside."

Despite their protests, I went to the box, and with my trusty pocket knife, had it open in a flash. Inside was a bright, shiny, brass ship's clock. My brother had threatened me with this for some time, but I had forgotten the promise and there was no particular occasion. The clock had simply arrived without warning. I thanked the officers, who were not amused, and took my new clock along with my chocolates and hand soap refill into the house where I poured a stiff Sherry to celebrate.

A Memorable Honeymoon

By Tom Brandt

George squeezed his wife's hand one more time. They had a wonderful marriage ceremony and now were headed off on their honeymoon. They had spent the first night in a hotel near the Miami airport where they had dinner in the room, and then a delicious consummation of their marriage. Now they were en route on the final leg of their journey to the British Virgin Islands where they expected a romantic hideaway.

The airplane banked into its final approach when it was buffeted by a sudden gust of wind. Their pilot poured on the fuel to maintain air speed as he lined up the landing approach. With the strong cross-wind he managed a hot landing. They bumped hard on the runway and then the engines roared with all the reverse thrust the pilot could manage to stop the plane on the short runway. The propeller-driven DC3 handled the emergency well.

Martha said, "George, that's the first time I've seen you white-knuckled while on a plane."

George said, "I guess this one was a little hard on the nerves."

He shook his head at his inane answer, but it was the best he could do. He'd flown many times, but the prop-jobs made him basically nervous. The squall-line hit the area as they stopped at the terminal.

Beef Island Airport building was not much bigger than a double garage. The covered baggage claim area lay next to the main structure. The crew waited for the worst of the storm to pass before opening the cabin door.

George and Martha made their way down the sloping floor and stepped onto the short ladder that led to the tarmac. Their luggage was already off the plane and waiting on the cart for the crew to move it into the shelter of the terminal. The baggage claim area had only a canopy covering it from the rain. George and Martha were soaked by the time they got to the waiting area and the safety of the hotel bus.

Once in the hotel lobby, they were guided to their rooms by an attentive bellman.

"Your luggage is already here," he said.

They moved into the room. George noticed a small puddle developing under their bags. They dismissed the bellman and opened their main suitcase. Martha shrieked with agony at the sight of her soggy trousseau. It seemed that the violent rain had penetrated the water-repellent barriers of her suitcase. Everything inside was sopping wet.

George was a bit luckier in that he had a mostly drip-dry wardrobe that could be hung in the bathroom. Still, drying would be a long process, given the high humidity of the Island climate.

They called the front desk clerk who sent a chambermaid. Together she and Martha pulled out her wettest items and the chambermaid took them and George's off to the hotel laundry. George looked at his wife and smiled as he said, "We should get out of these wet things. They need to dry too."

Martha hesitated, but then said, "Last one out is a rotten egg."

They laughed and stripped. Martha started to hang up her clothes, but George embraced her. They kissed and turned to the bed. George stripped off the counterpane and then the top sheet. Martha gasped, "OH NO!"

A large, hairy tarantula scampered across the pillow. George grabbed the other pillow as he swatted at the creature, but it darted away. He chased it across the living room to the window where it took refuge in the drapery. He swatted again, but the spider was quicker, scampering up the drape. George took another swipe and struck the drapery and the window with a mighty blow. With a loud crash the drape fell to the floor, curtain rod, sheers, and all. George stood momentarily, shocked by what he had done.

A covered corridor passed just outside his window, and beyond that a cocktail party had moved back outside, since the rain squall had passed on. He realized that he was in full view of the patrons attending the cocktail party, and he wore only a condom.

Martha, who wore even less, had dived behind the bed. George gathered his wits and collapsed onto the floor and crawled to the bed, where he gathered a blanket around himself. He disconnected a sheet, shook it to clear any spiders, and then tossed it to Martha. He then hobbled toward the light switches to turn off all the inside lights.

He had hoped that the window had the sun repellent film, but he had hoped in vain. He managed to drag the sofa away from the wall and position it with its back to the windows. Martha by now had wrapped herself in the sheet and crawled to meet him. They pulled the seat cushions from the sofa and lined them up on the floor, where they resumed their interrupted love making. As George savored the afterglow from a spectacular climax, he whispered, "Tomorrow has got to be a better day."

Together they giggled.

A Grizzly Bear

By Tom Brandt

It had been a great day for a hike. I had gone a couple miles with Jane, but I needed a rest. She was still full of it, so she went on without me. I had found a large Sequoia with an inviting root system to lie down for just a moment. I must have fallen asleep because I became aware of a lot of snuffling and scratching around. I opened one eye and saw not five feet from me a smallish bear. I shifted my gaze further out and saw another one. My drowsy mind started playing the child's nursery rhyme:

"If you go down to the woods today, you're in for a big surprise.

"If you go down to the woods today, you'd better go in disguise.

"Cause every bear that ever there was will gather there for certain.

"Because today's the day the teddy bears have their picnic."

EXCEPT!

These were not teddy bears. They were real live animals with fur and claws and teeth. Oh yes, these are little—probably born this last winter. OH SHIT! WHERE'S THEIR MOTHER? I raised my head far enough to see the great sow grazing on the other side of my clearing. I was in the worst possible position—between the sow and the cubs.

I looked around for a safe haven, but I didn't see much. There was a corpse a few yards to my left that the bears seem to be avoiding. I concentrated a bit more and woke up more of my senses. I caught the whiff of a familiar scent—skunk. Could that be my answer?

I couldn't think of anything else, so I crept slowly across the open ground until I had reached the corpse. The skunk was definitely at home. From this place I could see that the sow also had two yearling cubs in tow. By this time, the sow had noticed me and reared up on its hindquarters. Good God, she's big. I remembered not to run and stood up making myself as tall as I could. She made a grumbly sound in her throat and the cubs scurried directly to her and gathered behind her. The yearlings gathered close by, but off to one side. Clearly, they did not want to be associated with the little ones hiding behind their mother.

At this point my brain shifted into slow motion. The sow dropped to all fours and started across the clearing toward my corpse. She moved with massive dignity making low growls as she walked with a clear malicious intent. I stood braced to defend myself. I had twisted off a short stubby branch from the corpse which had disturbed the skunk enough to provoke a short spray.

The bear was nearly upon the corpse when it stopped with a shriek. It reared back and desperately pawed at its face. The earth shook with the force of its howls. It ran around the clearing blindly, running into small trees and other growth. Evidently the skunk had let fly with everything it had and caught the sow full in the face, temporarily blinding the great beast. The cubs and the yearlings all dithered with their mother. I seized the moment to quit the scene. I ran about a hundred yards, before I shifted into a dog-trot for the rest of the two miles to the parking lot.

Once in the relative safety of the parking lot, I took stock of my situation. I was winded, emotionally drained, and I stank. The skunk had got me after I pulled out the twig. I started to bewail my lot when I stopped in mid-thought. No. That's all wrong. Instead, I should celebrate my rescue from the sleuth of bears and thank God for including these stinky little critters in his creation.

Tropical Paradise

By Dorothy Enos

We landed on Maui at 1:00 pm. We flew directly from San Jose. Debbie and I had a beautiful Wedding Ceremony. Maui is a beautiful island. I thought Debbie would love it the same as I did, for it is "truly heavenly."

I drove a rental car to the hotel. The hotel was named "Paradise." No one was there to greet us. We thought that was strange, since the hotel looked nice from the outside. Flowers were blooming all over. Some of the flowers needed to be watered, though.

We walked into the hotel. The desk clerk was sound asleep in his chair. There was an empty vodka bottle on the floor. I walked around the desk to obtain a room key. I found one for room 6 and took it. We went down the hall to find the room.

I opened the door and found the room was smelly and dusty. We could hear voices above us. They were screaming and hollering, and drinking glasses were falling out of their windows onto the ground below.

I said to Debbie, "This is not a *tropical paradise*. This is false advertising."

We left and got in the car and I drove back to the airport. I went to the booking desk and ordered flight tickets back to San Jose.

As soon as we were in the air, we were flying home. The plane landed safely. We received our luggage, and I rented another car to take us to our home.

Debbie was soon in our house and said this is our paradise. We were so happy to be home. We went to Carmel for our honeymoon, and it was the perfect place. We are so happy now.

My Loveable Grandparents

By Dorothy Enos

My Grandparents on my Father's side were wonderful. I never knew my Mother's parents, for they passed away in the early 1900's. I had a great Mother, and her parents did a great job raising her, but the Grandparents that I'm writing about were my Father's parents.

Grandma's name was Marina and Grandpa's name was John. My sibling and I spent a lot of our early years with them, for we lost our Father in a farm accident, at a farm near King City.

Grandma was feisty and Grandpa was always calm and gentle. My Grandmother was a great cook. She was a good house keeper too. Her home always looked nice. She had a wash house, where she washed all her dirty clothes.

My mother would help Grandma when she could. Grandpa had a job at the grocery store. He delivered groceries to the local residents. He had a horse named Bozo, and he had a buggy which he pulled around. They would come by the house and pick me up. My siblings and I would climb up on the wagon. We rode with Grandpa as he delivered things. We had such a fun time.

Grandma kept a strict schedule for her meals. Breakfast was at 9:00 am, lunch at 12:00 noon, and supper at 6:00 pm, and she expected all of the family to be on time.

Grandma died at the age of 96 of natural causes. Grandpa died of a broken heart. His son, Uncle Rudy, joined the Army and left home. He and Grandpa were great pals when they were together.

In summary, I will always remember the time I spent with my wonderful Grandparents.

Henry

By Dorothy Enos

Henry's father died just before Henry was to enter Stanford University. He was now forced to run the family ranch instead. The house was a little adobe one, which he really loved. He decided not to go on to Stanford until things settled down.

Time went by and he was really enjoying his new life. He never did go to Stanford, and he was still on the ranch 80 years later. He had a pet dog, Bozzo, a little shepherd dog, and he had met a neighbor named Nellie.

They became good friends. Life was good. He had his book, his dog Bozzo, and his friend Nellie. At the age of 89, Henry passed away.

Nellie took Bozzo home with her. They both knew that Henry would be pleased while smiling down from heaven.

A Happy Place

By Dorothy Enos

I now live in a happy place. It is the Cedar Building at Atria. The reason I live here is due to my recent cancer surgery. My doctor said I should no longer live alone.

I love it here. The Med Techs and Care Givers are fantastic. Our building has 20 residents and we are like a family.

I participate in all of the activities, and have exercise every day at 10:00 am. The Activity Group from the main building has us do a lot of brain games.

My advice to you, if you want it, is that if you have to go to an assisted living facility, request Cedar. You won't be sorry.

We don't try to straighten out the world. There are no negative thoughts here. Some people try to have negative thoughts, but the rest of us put a stop to them.

I am the ambassador for Cedar. I talk with all new residents and I enjoy it very much. Life is good.

P.S. I am a lead singer in our choir on Tuesdays.

A Ghostly Adventure

By Dorothy Enos

The Ghostly family lived happily in the old house. They flew around all day, having so much fun. However, people were afraid to go near the house, for they were afraid of ghosts.

One day, as one of the ghosts was flying around downstairs, there were two little boys standing at the front door. One little boy said, "I wonder where our baseball is. We both saw it go through the window."

Their eyes were opened wide as a ghost flew around them, and the ball dropped in front of them. The boys were so happy. The ghost had seen a round thing on the floor that turned out to be the ball.

Bobby, one of the boys said, "You know, I'm not afraid anymore. The ghosts are very nice." One of the ghosts flew around the boys and smiled. Joey, the other boy said, "Yes, these ghosts seem to be very nice." The boys picked up the ball and left the house.

The Ghostly family was so happy with the adventure. Now neighbors will realize that people and ghosts can all be happy together. The ghost family will be looking forward to more days like this one.

The Tropical Non-Paradise

By Kent Humpal

"Honey, do you remember how we intended to take our honeymoon at a Tropical Paradise, but never had the money? Well, I found a way."

"What are you talking about?" asked Doreen.

"Well," Ian began his explanation, "I was in the café drinking a mocha cooler and I heard the people at the next table talking. They ran a reality trip show and it seems the couple they signed up had to drop out. They saw I was listening, so they started telling me about it. It sounded great and we would receive pay for it, as well."

"Something seems strange to me—kind of a folly," said Doreen.

"When I expressed an interest they began questioning me—you know, like was I married, do I have a long term relationship, do I have physical and medical conditions, and the like. I told them we had been married for three years and hadn't had a honeymoon and wanted to travel before we had any kids.

They gave me their cards with their numbers on them. I said I would talk to you about it. Allen, he seemed to be their boss, said they had to know in ten days, as the plane and chartered boat had already been signed up, and the money would be gone if they didn't get a couple to replace the drop outs. They do have another couple going to the same place, so it's not as if we would be all alone there."

After talking it over for a couple of days with Doreen bringing up many questions, Ian called the number on the card to set up a meeting. Going over all the questions raised by Doreen, plus some of the production company's terms and logistics of travel, Ian signed the agreement with the Adam and Eve Production Company, without any further input from Doreen.

"Well, honey, we're on our way. There were a few minor details like vaccinations to take, but Mr. Trunk assured me that none of their previous clients even caught a cold. There was a lot of gobble-de-gook in fine print, but they assured me it was the normal legalities of a company dealing with a foreign site. We have about five or six days to prepare things, so let's get started!

The next several days were filled with doctor's visits and checks on Visas and Passports which were mostly taken care of by the company's legal office. After arranging for Doreen's parents to take care of the dog and check the mail, Ian paid a few bills in advance, and they were now ready to go.

The company assured them they would provide everything they needed for tropical wear, and there would always be a film crew and production people around, so we should not worry.

A medium sized chartered plane flew them to Cancun Mexico, but they only stopped long enough to get onto a smaller plane that flew to Puerto Barrios on the Guatemalan Caribbean coast, a narrow stretch of coast line between Belize and Honduras.

They rested there for a day and waited for a boat with proper equipment to reach them. Delayed by a local squall, the boat arrived late that evening. The next morning they boarded a smaller, faster boat, and went up the coast to Livingston. Through Rio Dulce

National Park into Lake Herbal, the two couples and film crew were deposited at a neatly set up base camp on the northern shore. It was here that they actually met the second couple.

The second couple under contract was Taiwanese. Their names were Sauyong and Mailee Chow. They were a couple from Taiwan who spoke excellent English.

As they were unpacking, Doreen found the contract and browsed through it. Getting to the fine print gobble-de-gook that Ian had agreed with when he signed the agreement, she became alarmed.

"Honey, do you know what you signed us up for? You didn't even look at the special sections about clothing and what they expect from us."

"Well, they said they would supply clothing and any other items we would need to have in order to spend time in a secluded camp."

"Ian, do you know that you signed us up for a reality show—a rip-off of *Naked and Fearing*. It's called *Adam and Eve Out of the Garden*. I want out, tomorrow, so can we please talk to the producers to see what they can do for us?"

The next morning, before breakfast, Doreen confronted the two men. "Which one of you persuaded my husband to sign up for this fiasco? You should have known he would be taken in by your talk. I know he's gullible, but even he wouldn't have agreed to some of these provisions. Listen to some of what you have put into this contract which he signed."

> 1. Garments sufficient to cover the lower body from waist to thighs, with no inner-wear.
> 2. Toe and thong sandals.
> 3. Two items each couple must choose: a) a machete, b) an axe, c) a fire starter, d) a small pot, e) thin cords, f) some fish hooks, and g) a personal insect net.
> 4. Camera men and emergency staff will be with you at base camp for 24 hours.

"What about safety, emergencies, and modesty. Did my husband sign a disclosure agreement? It looks like we are going to be on International TV and the Internet."

"Well, Mrs. Marlow, can I call you Doreen? This is an iron-clad contract. The rights have all been sold and our agency and the sponsors have gone over this contract thoroughly. We did have some problems with the original show and our legal department

73

learned their lessons. Too bad, but you can't get out of it. You did notice penalty clauses didn't you?"

"Besides, the Chou's agreed to the contract and are ready to go!" the second man said.

Doreen caught up to Ian outside of the dining area. "The food is good and the cabins are small, but nice, and did you see the sky and lake. They are beautiful."

"Ian, did you see the penalty clauses. If we don't fulfill the contract or follow their directions precisely we have to pay for the full expenses of the trip— planes, boats, equipment, and cabin."

"So what, it's our honeymoon! It's our honeymoon and we can handle the plot. We stay out a couple of nights in a small camp in the forest, they film an adventure or two, and that's it—we go home."

"Ian, you dunce, we'll be out there for 8 to 10 days with fewer clothes than Jane and Tarzan, and with no Cheetah to amuse us. What do you think it meant to meet our needs, with proper camping equipment and camera people?"

"I said Dunce, but maybe fool or ignoramus would be a better description. We will each get essentially a loin cloth and two items from the list, and look it over. What do we want to choose?"

"But can't we share with the Chou's, each time with something different? Ian, I talked to them, and they are going to be on a different side of the lake. We will be miles apart. Can't we just refuse to cooperate, and bail out?"

"No, you idiot, we would have to pay for the trip, the equipment, and the production costs, which includes salaries and equipment rental. We would be in debt for years if we try to bail out now."

Leaving the Chou's the next morning miles up the shoreline where a small beach existed, Mailee waved tearfully as the boat left them behind with two cameramen and a meager amount of supplies, mostly for the crew. An hour later several miles up the densely forested shore, they motored part way up a small river where they were deposited at an opening in the rain forest, still dripping from an earlier rain.

The crew unloaded what looked to the Marlow's like a lot of good items—tents, camp stove, fresh and dried food, even a combination radio, which was set up.

"Mr. Watson, they were no longer on a first name basis, called them over. I'm glad you agreed to go through with this. The legal problems would have been nasty, and believe me you'll get by. You're in good shape, healthy, and very smart. Now, if you would just take off your clothes—no belts, no shoes, no caps. Here are your garments. I know they are skimpy but the audience likes that. We have to take your clothes, so you can't cheat. Besides we can see them on the footage."

Ian looked around, tore off a couple of strips from his loin cloth, made a belt out of it, and tied it up. Doreen flushed and finally dropped her clothes.

"Ian, this only covers me from the waist to my knees and barely includes knots at the side."

Then noticing the camera already filming, she moved to cover her only to have the loin cloth drop. The camera man called out. "You know, we blur out your breasts and crotch for TV, but of course that's done in the studio, not here."

The rest of the afternoon they scouted a camp site and using the machete Ian and I selected they made a rudimentary shelter. Doreen finally got a fire going using her Girl Scout knowledge from long ago.

Recriminations began the next day. "You let the fire go out! Well, it was out anyway, but smoke kept some of the insects off. If you would let me take the fish-hooks, I could have used the vines as a line and maybe caught us some breakfast. What would we give up, the machete or the fire kit," asked Doreen.

As the argument came to an inconclusive status, they realized they were being filmed by a crew member munching a burrito filled with egg, bacon, and salsa. A cup of his coffee sat on a near-by rock.

The next couple of days were spent looking for a better campsite, a better water source, and more food. Ian surprised himself and Doreen by making a habitable lean-to against a rock face. Outer facing branches and large leaves woven together with vines kept most of the sporadic showers out and off of them. They soon learned that biting insects didn't like the rain, so it was the best time to forage and hunt. Surviving on somewhat familiar fruit and what the local monkeys were eating off the trees and bushes they made it through the first two days.

Ian overcame his squeamishness and was able to kill a couple of median sized Iguanas. Gutting them and skinning the meat was a new experience for what were two city folk. They decided it didn't taste like chicken, but it was good anyway.

Meanwhile they could smell the food cooked by the crew and debated raiding their camp during the night. That idea was tossed aside when they heard Jaguar growls and grunts in the night and found his or her left overs not far away, surrounded by some imposing paw tracks.

Getting through the next few days, they agreed they had survived better than they thought they would, even getting used to being almost naked in front of strangers with cameras. Also they both had lost weight and realized that they had probably been living a very sedentary life. With all of this they were looking forward to getting out. The pickup was only a couple of days away.

The next morning Steve and Ron came hurrying up from their camp. They were no longer anonymous, but if not friends, at least friendly companions.

"Ian, Doreen, we have some bad news. We just received a wireless message from Mr. Warren. They won't be able to get us out on time—in fact they don't know when they will be able to get us out. They picked up the Chou's late last night, but a tropical storm has hit Livingston, stopping boat traffic and not allowing small planes to take off. They can't get to us now for a while.

"Damn it, we were really looking to get out—you guys know we did our best. Doreen spoke up. "Are you guys going to keep filming? It's going to be nasty and maybe dangerous for all of us, not just Ian and me."

"Well, think about it. If we film at least the beginning of the storm and how you two cope with it, you could probably squeeze some more money out of them by threatening a law suit, etc. Ron says we can probably get overtime or a better contract for next time if we have gotten some scene showing dangerous situations or whatever."

Ian and Doreen huddled together. "OK, but we have some requests. Between filming we share clothes, stoves, whatever you have left and we help you prepare. We're pretty good now, but you know that."

Filming the next few days showed the two preparing the shelter, reinforcing the poles and leaves, collecting fire wood, and foraging for food that would keep. Ian even killed a large rodent that Steve thought was a Capybara. It was big enough to last several days, if rationed. By the time the storm hit they had incorporated parts of the tent to strengthen the shelter and shoved the stove and remaining food into the enlarged shelter.

The storm was beyond all their imaginations. What they had seen on TV had not prepared them for the winds driving the rain sideways, upwards, around and blowing anything not weighted or tied down off to who knows where. Even with the rain gear shared among them, they were soaked and shivering.

The third morning the storm began to blow itself out and by noon was virtually gone. By 2:00 they heard the power boat coming up the river. Hurrying down the path to the river, with help from the crew, the four of them, now friends by adversity loaded everything into the boat. Arriving back at Livingston a few hours later they moved into the cabin.

People in town arranged for them to call home. They discovered family and friends had been alerted by the Guatemalan and US authorities. The company had done basically nothing for them. The Chou's were gone, back home to Taiwan, non-the worse for their adventure.

Warren was back in Florida. They caught him talking to another couple in the outer office. "Well, you made it back all right. I heard good reports on the footage. Everyone is happy with how you performed. We will cut out the last scenes when you were wearing borrowed shorts and a T-shirt. We won't penalize you for that."

It took both Ian and a security guard to pry Doreen off of him. He was sputtering red, and gasping for breath when they left.

"Gosh, honey, you couldn't have done that before the trip—you really got stronger. You could have him down and out in a few more seconds. If he hadn't said that about the penalties, I was going to ignore him, but I knew he had been ogling me on the uncut film when he said that. I just lost it."

Their Attorney forced the company into accepting an additional settlement for the hazardous situation and slow response. It turned out that they had plenty of warning time to evacuate both the Chou's and the Marlowe's, but had decided the storm provided better and more exciting film.

The Russian Refugee

By Kent Humpal

Refugee! What did that mean? He had no country. His family had fled Eastern Russia during the Bolshevik take over. Middle class merchants, dealers in European imports—mostly clothing, jewelry, maybe some luxury smuggled items, perfume, silk stockings, and wine—nothing too big. The family had supported the men's endeavors, but then lost their business and finally their home.

Their father had fought with the White army in Siberia, finally ending up with the American expeditionary force, as a translator/aide. As everything collapsed and fell apart, the remaining family escaped into Manchuria. Father, Mother, Sister Irene, and Brother Vasalenko Smolinsky, made it into Japanese-held territory. We never knew what happened to my older brother, Gregorovitch, fighting with the Republican Legion along the rail lines. There were so many different groups fighting and infighting that we were never sure where he was.

We settled in Harbin, a major trade and travel center, and struggled to make a living like most of the exiles did. We survived the first year by selling jewelry that my mother had hidden away. I worked for a Chinese trading company as the lowest clerk, and my sister taught Russian and British English to Chinese and Japanese merchants.

Eventually my father re-established some connections with other exiles in Europe, especially in France. We never made it back to luxury, but we lived reasonably well by pooling our money. There was a large Russian exile population in Harbin. Most of us, the younger population, recognized that even if we returned to Russia, now called the Soviet Union, we would never regain what we had lost. Some of the older generation, still hoping, continued to plot and connive, but after some unexpected deaths among the leaders, things were resolved into unhappy grumbling.

Manchuria, under Japanese control, became Manchukuo with a puppet government, the last

Chinese Emperor ruling under Japanese military control. It made no difference, however, for our status—we were still stateless non-citizens, but the Japanese connection gave us some difference. Russia was a mutual enemy, but we were still pawns in a game we couldn't play.

We kept our status quo during WW II. Japan and the Soviets remained armed and ready but never did declare war. We began to collect jewelry and items readily exchangeable again.

My mother passed on old business tricks before passing away in the night. My father, dying not long afterwards, had us commit names and places in Europe and the US to memory. My sister had married a man with Swedish papers and diplomatic ties, and his family with two children went back to Sweden with the fall of Germany, where they were safe.

In August, 1945, a massive bomb was dropped on Japan. As a consequence, the word was out that the Japanese Army was withdrawing to the home islands. We were considered being Russian, and we knew what would happen to us if the Red army invaded us. We had been preparing for the eventuality.

We hired or bribed a captain of a small ship. He had a dubious nationality, and a barely sea worthy vessel. He claimed neutrality, and for good measure he had papers and flags from Spain, Portugal, and Sweden. It was our best chance.

Crowding onto a train full of Japanese and other multiethnic refugees, we made it to Dairen. Flying a Portuguese flag, we zig zagged into a small harbor in China. Interned by the Nationalist forces we were kept in a camp until the US officials granted us refugee status.

Today I live in San Francisco, part of a large Russian neighborhood. Now I am a US citizen, an American born wife with two children, Natalya and Gregory. I am no longer a non-person.

The Long Term Sub

By Kent Humpal

Mr. Ferratoo came into the classroom slowly, blinking, and squinting in the florescent lighting. It was the beginning of the second quarter and he was replacing the regular teacher. She had rather unexpectedly become ill with some sort of blood disorder.

The students, looking him over, were not sure what to make of him—hair, dark brown, and a little on the longish side, but styled. His eyes were light brown but as some would notice later, they became almost amber when he was in the sunlight, and most of the time they were covered by aviator style sunglasses, even indoors.

He dressed well, even if a little dramatically, in suits that were somewhat out of style. He was friendly, but a little restrained. Those who talked to him thought they detected a slight eastern European accent. Several endorsed him because he volunteered to take the dreaded night time activities off their hands, such as football games, dances, and certain other evening performances.

Many of the younger teachers cultivated his friendship, seeing him as more sophisticated and cultured than they. Teaching English/European literature and drama, he attracted a mixture of the better students and many of the Goth culture.

Staying after school for the drama groups, he began tutoring some of them. The group began to shrink as some began to suffer from fatigue and eating disorders. Some of the group even began to lose concentration and frequently dozed off. Most parents attributed it to stress from the high expectations of the students themselves. At the same time, many of his students seemed to thrive on the work and routine. Consequently, he looked rejuvenated, less drawn, and less sallow.

The twice yearly blood drive was about to enter its second session. As he had back-to-back prep sessions at the end of each day, Mr. Ferratoo agreed to supervise the drive. The administration was happy to have someone so willing to take over. When asked about it he said, "Well, I don't faint at the sight of blood, and it certainly is a necessity for life. I know many people who depend on the blood banks for a living, so I am glad to help."

Although run by the local blood banks and the Red Cross, Mr. Ferratoo was responsible for sign-ups, scheduling, and monitoring of all donations. Several of his friends had previously volunteered for similar events. Working in emergency rooms, and on emergency response teams, they all agreed to help out.

The first sessions in the fall had gone well, but a series of traffic accidents and exceptionally brutal and bloody muggings and robberies had led local agencies to seek greater contributions of blood than usual. There had been some discrepancies in the first accounting—more donors than blood stocks counted—that was credited to waste and inefficiency, but this time the groups vowed to be more watchful.

Each day began uneventfully—donors trickled in, soothed by the muted lighting and soft music, and then given apple juice and donuts for energy, before returning to class. Mr. Ferratoo was in and out

89

periodically—checking on students and their progress, while conferring with some of his friends.

By mid-afternoon, students not recovering from giving blood quickly began to lodge complaints, with word beginning to circulate by phone and tweeted comments. Some students said they had dozed off, a general problem, when more blood than usual was taken. They said that they felt weak and light headed.

As the messages came to the attention of the Assistant Principal, Ms. Vanna Helsing, she became worried that something was wrong. There were too many weary and emotional students coming into the office. In addition, the groundskeeper, Emmanuel, came to her to report seeing disturbing activities around the portable where the donations were being collected.

"Ms. Helsing, a black van is picking up ice chests from the donor sites. Some of the people were conferring with Mr. Ferratoo, but everything going on was hasty and kind of secretive. I asked Mr. Ferratoo about it later and he said that they needed it immediately because of a bad accident, but Ms. Helsing, I kept my radio and scanner on, and nothing was reported."

"Thanks, Emanuel, I think something funny is going on too, and you've given me a clue as to what it is," replied Ms. Helsing.

Walking slowly to an area where she could observe the comings and goings of the donors and check on her list of volunteers, she became aware of two things. There were more volunteers than were listed and the donors were in the place for ten to fifteen minutes longer than they should have been.

She edged to the back of the area and checked out the loading area. There were the usual Red Cross and local blood bank vans, but also an unmarked vehicle was parked nearby.

Intercepting a couple of students leaving the area with orange juice, she spoke quietly, "Did you boys notice anything different, maybe unusual while you were in there?"

A sturdy athletic looking one replied. "Well, after getting some weird text from a couple of friends, I was watching for something unusual, but I kind of dozed off. I was there longer than I was supposed to be, but I thought they were just letting me recover longer. It was funny. The rest of us got orange juice or apple juice, but some of the guys were drinking v8 from a

91

large glass pitcher." He continued. "I think Charlie here looked more pale than usual, but he always looked pale to me."

Charlie spoke up. "I thought some of the helpers were kind of strange. They looked kind of pale, and didn't smile or talk with us like the others did, you know, to kind of settle us down to reduce our fears."

Vanna went to get the school nurse. Ms. Morales observed the giving of the donations to see if anything seemed different, and she came back looking disturbed.

"Something is going on, and that's for sure. They obviously are side tracking some of the blood. Maybe they are selling it on the black market."

The police liaison, Mr. Lance Boyle, met with Principal Pat Ernesto, who had agreed to call the police. Tracking them led the group to a dark abandoned warehouse near the building. The van was driven into the dark interior, and even in the dim light the police could see a strange crew placing bags and bottles of blood into a large refrigeration unit. The workers were of several ages and ethnic groups. They all looked unnaturally sallow no matter what their skin color was.

As the police turned on their spotlights, many of the group flinched and covered their eyes or sought the darkest corners of the area they were in.

Back at the school the word spread about the unusual goings on at the blood drive. The situation began to take a bizarre and dramatic turn of events.

Mr. Ferratoo confronted by Vanna Helsing, Lance Boyle, Principal Ernesto, and Emanuel with back up from the cafeteria staff loaded down with garlic garlands and assorted crucifixes smiled for the first time, showing off a fine set of fangs.

"What's all the fuss? Have you organized a Comic con or re-enactment group? Where are the torches and pitch-forks?"

Principal Ernesto spoke up. "We've become aware of some unusual practices in the blood donations you were supervising this year and we would like some explanations. There were shortages in the previous donations and yet in this year more blood has been drawn than contracted for by the blood banks. The police have found a storage site on the edge of town where an un-licensed staff is moving the excess blood. What do you have to say about this? You seem to be the organizer."

Removing his reflective sunglasses, Mr. Ferratoo replied, "Am I being charged with a crime? Am I being dismissed without a hearing? Do I need an attorney or my Union representative?"

Miss Vanna Helsing, giving him a piercing look spoke up. "My family has a history of tracking down your kind. You're a vampire aren't you? I wish I had sensed it sooner. You are going to be exposed, charged, and dismissed. I wish I had the right to destroy you right now."

Mr. Ferratoo began to show his agitation. "Wait a minute. Please let me explain some things to you."

A local detective arriving on the scene called out, "Back Off. Let's hear what he has to say. I may need to read him his rights."

"Ok, let me clarify some things," Mr. Ferratoo said. "First of all I have been granted asylum as a minority by your immigration authorities and given permanent refugee status. You don't know how my kind have been tormented and destroyed through the centuries. Mrs. Helsing's family has been particularly persistent. They've harassed us in every country where we tried to settle down in."

94

"But you are vile, and evil, and you destroy the very humanity and soul in mankind," cried Ms. Helsing.

"There are bad people in every group—not all of us prey upon humans, declared Mr. Ferratoo. My group of helpers is all here legally. They have visas from all over the world, wherever we are hated and threatened. The blood bank is legally certificated and only accepts animal blood or human averages. It's also recognized as a specialty blood bank by the state."

After several meetings with local, state, and Federal authorities, followed by public hearings and crowds of protestors on both sides, the situation migrated to the back pages of a tabloid, as a group of cannibals came forth to state their goals for acceptance. In the aftermath Ms. Vance Helsing and Principal Pat Ernesto made the rounds of the talk shows, and all participants were interviewed repeatedly and contacted by the TV networks and movie producers.

Mrs. Helsing's book on her family and the recent affair with Mr. Ferratoo became a miniseries on cable, while Mr. Ferratoo finished teaching adult night school. He is presently negotiating for a hosting position on a network talk show.

Interviewed while filming a commercial for a dental implant and orthodontist group, Mr. Ferratoo said, with a gleam in his eyes and an open smile, "I'm staking my future on this opportunity."

The Ghosts in the Haunted House

By Kent Humpal

They were a strange pair. They shared different ethnicities, languages, and backgrounds, plus the fact that their deaths had been almost one hundred years apart. They met in what is called the after-life. Dead by accident, one was killed and buried by a grieving loving family member, while the other was buried by Mother Nature.

Efraim Meyerbeck was eternally ten years old—his companion had taken his own name, following Indian tradition. He now called himself *Young Man Looking Thru Shadows*, but to Efraim he was Manny, his kind of friend. Manny was like Efraim, set at one age, somewhere in his middle teen years.

Circumstances had thrown them together at this singular site, a toy store in what had become California. Manny had passed while running from the mission padres. Separated from his family, and relegated to menial farm tasks, he longed for the freedom of his tribal relatives, who were still living in the eastern foothills of the valley in small family groups. A misstep in the night, a tumble down a gulley, followed by the striking of his head on a boulder, had brought him almost instant death. Also the flashed floods of the spring had buried him deeply under a carved off cut bank.

Efraim's death came about 100 years later. Escaping or fleeing from the dust bowl disasters of the 30s, his family left Arkansas for California, looking for relief from the loss of their rented farms. They were lumped in with the Okies, but let people know that they came from Arkansas, not Oklahoma—a subtle, but meaningful difference to them.

While his folks and Uncle Albert worked in the dairies and orchards in the valley, he was left to entertain himself. Albert was only a few years older, but had carved a wooden boat and a toy pistol for Efraim out of soft wood.

The creek where he was playing, swollen by late rains, was swift and muddy. Chasing his prized boat downstream, Efraim, like Manny, stumbled, fell, and drowned, clutching his toy boat and pistol in his hands. With no money and not wanting to stay where the tragedy took place, the family buried him in an out of the way corner of the camp. A small marker carved by his uncle stood for a few months, then disappeared.

They discovered that there were no language barriers in the spirit world. There were no ailments, no hunger, no heat, or cold. No need for sleep, or obeying rules or commands, either—just existence. There was no haunting, per se. If something or someone was interested, then they would appear.

Sometimes at chilly spots, unexplained breezes, occasionally even ephemeral images. There were an unimaginable number of items, especially toys that intrigued and sometimes entertained them. They took part sometimes when children pulled things from the shelves—each generation demonstrated the newest toys.

Only at night did they try out things themselves. Employees began noticing misplaced toys, noises, disturbances in the air, even an occasional glimpse of spectral bodies. Rumors and stories spread. As they were neither malevolent nor malicious, most workers didn't care. Skeptics and believers sought them out and left with their own beliefs unaltered.

Efraim and *Young Man Looking Thru Shadows* were bound together in death as they would never have been in life. With nothing to prove and nothing to gain, they would be companions until released. They would remain immune to earthly vagaries.

The Big Bad Wolf

By Kent Humpal

After the run in with the wild, axe-waving woodsman, the Big Bad Wolf decided to get out of the burglary and mugging trades. The last event had been a set up anyway. Red Riding Hood had obviously been an under-cover name. He should have known better, for there were doughnuts in her basket and she was carrying a cup of Peets coffee.

Not the usual fare one carried to an older grandmother. When they got to the woods she stopped at each clearing, pausing to look around. When he got out of the brush, instead of the nice sweet dog talk—what big ears, eyes and teeth, etc., she blew a whistle and his ears still hurt, and she hauled out a can of wolf repellant.

Boy, he broke for the brush just in time to avoid the so-called woodsman. One look back and I knew.

He had a bushy beard and plaid shirt, and a belt that held a tazer. Only the fact that he grabbed a doughnut from the basket and clicked on his body camera could give me the chance to escape. The captors were no good in the forest and he knew the side trails. Once he got away he decided that was it. He would stick to sheep and pigs from now on.

My Grandmother

By Christine Jones

I grew up with my grandmother living with us, while my parents struggled to survive in Post War II Poland. She always had time for me. She was tiny, often dressed in long black dresses, and told me many tales of life under the Russian Tsar.

Our part of Poland was taken over by Russia at the end of the 18th century, when Poland ceased to exist as a separate country. It was divided into three parts — Russia, Austria, and Prussia, and was reborn again in 1918, at the end of World War I, when President Wilson insisted on its emergence.

Life in the newly emerged Poland was difficult for most people. It emerged as it did with great income inequality and was run by aristocrats. Grandma spoke nostalgically of life under the Tsar. Life in Poland was easier and more pleasant. People had plenty of money made of pure gold. The common complaint of the times was that it was too heavy to carry.

She also talked of faraway America, the land of milk and honey, and of the fierce people who lived there—the American Indians. She even told me a number of Indian prophesies. She did not identify them as such. It was only after she came to the USA and became interested in Indians and their prophesies that I realized I had heard them all before from grandma.

She had extensive knowledge of fairy tales, both Polish and Russian, and I never got tired of listening to them. Many of the fairy tales had sad endings that made me cry, so she would kindly change the endings to make me happy.

All this happened when I was very young. As we both grew older I developed other interests, but I always felt that she was on my side and I could count on her support. Around her also developed the first conflict in my life that I can remember. Looking back I can understand what the problem was. Then I just felt confused and guilty.

The struggle was over my father. He was the youngest, her baby, and very charming. Both she and my mother both wanted his love and affection. Mother complained a great deal about grandma and sometimes forbade me to spend much time with her. I loved them both and felt often that I was betraying one or the other. Grandma died just as we were going to leave for the USA.

She gave me so much unconditional love, developing imagination, and the possibility of a wider and more exciting world and the belief that all was possible.

Against the Wrong Wall

By Christine Jones

I never thought that I would get old. I pursued the American dream of success with great passion. The effort took all of my time. I never asked if that was what I really wanted. The admiration that I received was enough.

I had many friends and went to lots of parties. Life seemed good, but slowly trouble crept in. Life got dull, boring, and required more and more parties, more and more cocktails. Our lifestyle became more extreme. We forgot who we were and what we wanted. We believed that as long as the invitations continued, and we went to fun events, we were fine.

Sometimes when I was alone, which was seldom, I thought about the serious child that served as an altar boy at my parish, how I loved God, how I felt that God loved me, and how I wanted to serve him.

I would quickly chase such thoughts away with another cocktail. Finally it was my wife who broke the spell we were under. My wife decided that she did not love me, but she still loved my money. She concentrated on keeping as much of it as she could. Maybe money would ward off the old age, poor health, and the end of the life that was coming.

I still wanted my old life back, clinging to the illusion that it was possible, when my daughter, who I hardly knew, sought to gain total control of me and my money. I refused to believe it. I finally woke up and noticed that the ladder I was climbing was against the wrong wall and that the wall was crumbling.

I found that my friends magically disappeared, and there was nobody to help me. My wife and daughter acted like they wanted me dead. I had nothing left, not even the money I gave up. I can now see that they robbed my money and my freedom.

I feel like it is mostly my fault. I never examined the wall that I put my ladder on. I now think that King Solomon was right, when he said that all life is vanity and blows away with the wind. The only values worth pursuing, I now know, are service to others, self-development, and the love of God and others.

About Cuba

By Christine Jones

I came to the USA in 1959, the year the Cuban Revolution ended, when the Communists won. I spoke no English and therefore never heard much about it. In Poland the revolution was not covered by the press. In 1962 there was the Cuban Missile crisis, and by that time I knew enough English to become interested.

Before the revolution, Cuba was run by President Juan Batista, a dictator. The island was run like the American mafia, in the style of Las Vegas. The President and the system were corrupt and were despised by the common people, who lived in great poverty.

The story interested me and I wanted to go to Cuba and see things for myself. That's when I found out to my great surprise that while in Poland, you could not leave the country, nor if you were in the USA, you could not go to some countries such as Cuba. So the idea of visiting Cuba went to my back burner for a long time.

A few years ago I finally had a chance to go to Cuba legally. The trip had the approval of the State Department and was in some way connected to the Smithsonian Institute. The experience was like traveling back in time. Almost all of the cars were from the 50's, as I remembered them, and the roads were amazingly empty. We traveled to the coast from Havana, a trip of several hours, and only saw one car going in the opposite direction.

The people on the trip were all American and for some reason they all seemed to be afraid of starving, so they brought lots of food with them, with a heavy emphasis on peanut butter. They were greatly disappointed, however, for there was no starvation. We were very well fed.

The basic food was sold for a minimal price or was given away for free to the people. University education and medical care were also free, and the people seemed happy and they liked Fidel Castro.

Coming from a communist country I had an eye for propaganda and there was very little. The Cubans liked the fact that Fidel's children were not interested in taking over and running the country. They were well educated and they worked outside of the government. A discussion was going on always as to who would take over after Fidel.

Cuba was visibly a poor country, at least partly due to the world-wide embargo enforced by the USA, and the buildings were old and in a state of disrepair. However there were none of the common sights seen in South America shanty towns, such as begging and homeless children.

While my visit in Cuba was limited in both scope and time, I talked to many local people as well as to several Canadians who came each year, and they agreed with my observations. The island was supported financially by the Soviet Union, which had become apparent after the USSR fell apart in 1991. The result was a flood of boat people who were starving, without the food from Russia.

Castro partially solved the problem by trading the well-educated Cuban doctors for oil with Venezuela and for pushing a drive for food production in Cuba.

111

With that, the boat people stopped coming to the island.

When the Revolution first started in 1953, many of the wealthy left the island, leaving many of their possessions hidden behind double walls in their buildings, for they believed that the revolution would fail in a few weeks, and they would be back then.

In the past several years there have been many changes in Cuba. People are now allowed to open restaurants and some small businesses. We had some great food and great music, and there is no advertising. The country is beautiful, as are the beaches. All the American food was left behind. I never asked the Cubans if they liked peanut butter.

Dag Hammarskjold's Death

By Dorothy Madden

I have been at times enraptured, awed, and sobered by the life of Dag Hammarskjold, Swedish diplomat, economist, and author who served as the Secretary-General of the United Nations from April 1953 to September 1961.

His book, *Markings*, has been called by the New York Times "perhaps the greatest testament of personal devotion published in this century." The manuscript of this book was found among his belongings after his death with a note to Leif Belfrage, permanent Under-Secretary for Foreign affairs, which says, among other things, that it is a diary that he has kept for many years.

It was not written for anyone but himself, but his later history and after all that has been said and written about him he began to see that perhaps after his death there would be interest. So he says, "If you find them (the entries) worth publishing you have my permission to do so—as a sort of white book concerning my negotiations with myself—and with God."

These entries as he comes to terms with his struggle to discover what his life's calling should be are enthralling and interesting. Hammarskjold himself says, "They were signposts you began to set up after you had reached a point where you needed them, a fixed point that was on no account to be lost sight of."

And most probably this "fixed point" is described in the entry for White Sunday 1961 when he writes, "But at some moment I did answer *yes* to someone— or something—and from that hour on I was certain that existence is meaningful and that, therefore, my life, in self-surrender, had a goal."

Between ten and fifteen minutes after midnight on Monday, September 18, 1961, a DC-6KB aircraft crashed near the airport of Ndola, a town in the British colony of Northern Rhodesia (now Zambia), not far from the Congo border. The plane had flown from Leopoldville (now Kinshasa) and was taking Dag Hammarskjold and his entourage on a mission to

114

try to bring peace to the Congo. Only one of the 16 people aboard, the Chief of Security, was found alive and he died six days later.

I have some questions for Dag Hammarskjold if I could in some other life perhaps meet with him:

1. Why did you have no burns when the other victims were badly burned and charred?

2. How did you escape the intense blaze which destroyed 75 to 80 percent of the fuselage?

3. Were you alive when you were shot? The hole seen in your forehead was removed from the autopsy reports and the reports themselves were removed from the case files.

Controversy over the cause of the crash continues still to this day. Maybe the official verdict "pilot error" will be changed as a result of new investigations some day.

A book, written in 2014 by Susan Williams, entitled *"Who killed Dag Hammarskjold, The UN, The Cold War, or The White Supremacy in Africa,"* is a fascinating read about one of the outstanding mysteries of the 20th century. I quote from a blurb about the book:

"At the heart of this book is Hammarskjold himself—a courageous and complex idealist, who sought to shield the newly independent nations of the world from the predatory instincts of the Great Powers. It reveals that the conflict in the Congo was driven not so much by internal divisions as by the Cold War and by the West's determination to keep real power from the hands of the post-colonial governments of Africa. It shows, too, that the British settlers of Rhodesia were ready to maintain white minority rule at all costs."

My favorite of the many quotes I love from his book, *Markings*, is "For all that has been *thanks*, for all that will be *yes!*"

Hacking

By Dorothy Madden

It was in September that she first noticed the money appearing on her statements. The first one was for $500. There was no familiar entry for it. A few days later, just when she was intending to call or visit the bank, a second deposit appeared on the statement. This one was for an additional $1,000.

Okay, something is royally screwed up here. She decided to take her statements that she had printed out into Charlene, the very helpful personal assistant at Chase Bank. Charlene looked at the statements and began to trace them. Apparently it was deposited from a foreign country—that was it—no name or number, just some foreign country.

Vanya was becoming increasingly worried about his mother, Dorothea. Their relationship was a warm and loving one, except for one important issue that divided them—his job. He was employed as a computer specialist in a large anonymous Russian company. His specialty was hacking and he was very good at his job—so good in fact that he had just received a sizable bonus for a major job he had completed.

It was in all the papers and he felt excited when he thought of his participation. He brought his mother some flowers to celebrate. She was thoughtful when he came home for dinner with them and asked about what it was that he was celebrating. For the first time he noticed how frail she had become and he suddenly became alarmed.

She asked him if he had any idea who the people were he was stealing from. Just rich Americans he had said. She persisted and asked if he had a name and information about any of them. Boastfully he said he knew pretty much everything about them—their Social Security Number, their date of birth, their family information, and so forth. Her response was essentially the same as before, but he noticed that she was less agitated, but just as firm.

What he was doing was wrong. He was injuring innocent people she said, and someday he will regret his actions and possibly be caught. He brushed off her objections as he always did, gently with a bit of humor, and said he was going out for a drink with Boris when he finished dinner.

When he returned and entered the living room, Dorothea was in a chair and had apparently been reading, for the lamp was still on, leaving a circle of gold on her book. She was still warm, but definitely was dead when he hugged her and wept.

His days and nights blurred into one, as he arranged for what had to be done next. My life will never be the same, he thought, and sometime in the next week the idea came to him how to honor his mother.

He hacked into the data he had collected and found a woman his mother's age and name and looked at everything about the stranger named Dorothy, whose life he had recently up ended. Carefully he deposited money into her banking account, hiding details to protect himself. Sometimes he would say to himself as he did so "this is from Dorothea." Somehow these acts brought his mother closer to him as he navigated his new life alone. The last time he said "I'm leaving this job now but if I get caught giving money to Dorothy before I leave, it will be your fault, Mom." He smiled to himself as he thought of her probable response. "I hope not, my darling Vanya."

Late-Life Love

By Dorothy Madden

She moved into a retirement residence after her husband of 40 years died of complications of congestive heart failure. It was a long and difficult goodbye. Her daughters had picked out the residence, and helped with the move from a large home into a 900 sq. ft. two-bedroom apartment. Losses all around—husband, home, piano, dear familiar furniture. She knew she could not stay there and told herself to plan to move in six months and to use this time to get well.

She went to individual and group grief counseling and struggled to get off depression and anti-anxiety medications. She was hospitalized with a possible heart attack. She felt lost, lonely, and frightened of exactly what she didn't know.

After months she began to make friends at dinner and lunches and began to adjust to community living. One such friend was a man who shall remain nameless who had also been married for a long time and had been widowed for five years. He was also acquainted with grief.

He had been married for 50 years and took care of his wife the last 15 years of her life as the disease progressed. As it turned out their kids knew each other as teenagers from the Saratoga Presbyterian Church Youth Group of which she was teacher/advisor some 40 years ago. He was helpful and kind, sharing how he handled the death of his wife. Slowly she began to heal.

More months passed and he began to become more important in her life. He made her feel beautiful and made her laugh which was enough at first. They were both surprised and a bit bewildered at how young they both felt when together. How can I be so smitten at age 83 she asked herself? But it was so much fun to feel joyful again that she stopped questioning her feelings and just relaxed into what she now began to call love.

The heart has its reasons that reason knows nothing of, said Pascal. Now, after almost two years together, it has deepened into a richer love, a deeper passion. She is still smitten and when she begins to analyze things, which is how she operates, she realized that they have consciously attempted to honor the rhythms and patterns of each other's life, adjusting when necessary to the unique ways the other is in the world and in the relationship.

She credits candor, patience, a willingness to talk things out, and an acceptance of what cannot be changed as to why it is so good.

She once said to him, "I don't understand how we can feel so young. We're both old."

He held her and said, "Yes, we are old, but so what? We're together and we'll grow older together."

She then recalled part of Robert Browning's poem, *"Grow old along with me, the best is yet to be, the last of life for which the first was made."*

"I'll take it," she said.

They will be married in May.

<u>*On Regrets*</u>

By Dorothy Madden

After a day of hiking, I showered and dressed for dinner and joined other folks in the restaurant of Tanaya Lodge where I was staying. Savoring my glass of wine while waiting for the entrees, as I usually do, my glance travelled around the restaurant, observing the other diners.

I noticed a group at a nearby large table. There was an elderly lady, a young boy probably of high school age, and three couples. Judging from the conversation, flowing happily between the couples fortified by glasses of wine, I gathered it was a reunion and everyone was in happy spirits. As I observed them I noticed that there were attempts from whom I presumed to be the mother to interject some comment or two, only to be nicely but firmly shut down by "Oh, yes, Mom," and quickly went back to the conversation.

They continued to reminisce of their childhood memories and growing up times with different versions being debated and laughed about. After one or two attempts to join in, the mother grew silent. She only spoke quietly and occasionally to the boy who responded unenthusiastically.

That little tableau has stayed with me for years, and now I find myself in that same situation occasionally when my adult children gather. When children are young you are at the center of their lives but as they grow older you are often moved to the periphery of their lives as it should be. I recall the saying that a good therapist is like a parent (if you do a good job, your clients or children grow up and leave you). But are we ever prepared to be left out?

I have tried to remember if I ever did this to my own mother. I probably did with no sense of how thoughtless I was being. I'm sorry, Mama.

Prompt Response

By Dorothy Madden

Liam stood quietly at the edge of the grazing area and took a deep breath in. How lucky he was to have found this job. He was sure that the fact that his uncle knew the owner of the Park helped. The family joked about his love for animals and how he ran away, not to join the circus, but to work with animals at the wild Animal Safari Park.

It was true—he had always loved animals and seemed to have a way with them. Now at 17 and just entering his last year of high school he had decided to spend this last summer here at the Park before choosing a college, in order to think a bit about what was best for him.

Being a veterinarian occurred to him, but he didn't think his grades were good enough to get into vet school. Anyway he didn't want to think about that now. He'll put that away until after summer.

He took another deep breath, but this time it felt different. Smoke! But where was it coming from? He noticed the animals moving nervously in the grazing field and they were coming together. Just then a pick-up truck came barreling down the road and Ken, the driver and the other person working in the Park yelled "the ridge is on fire and it's coming our way. We have to get the animals to safety somehow."

But Liam thought how? Hasty consultations among the men came up with a plan to bring up the big park trailer and load all the smaller caged animals onto the trailer and move it to the far edge of the park. They also decided to dig trenches around the grazing area and move the grazing animals to the center. He didn't let himself think the thought that this could be a real disaster if they didn't hurry.

They then hooked up all the hoses they had to the water faucets and wet the field down as best they could. Liam felt the adrenalin as he swung into action. He called his uncle and the owner who had just heard the news and they said that they and the fire trucks were on the way.

Liam had another problem. A month or so ago they found a small abandoned black bear. His mother had been killed just after the baby was born. Liam took the baby and nursed it using a bottle and round-the-clock feedings. They were rarely apart, but now with all the work to be done, Liam could not hold him as he used to.

He and Ken decided to improvise so they made a backpack contraption and tucked little Barney in it and strapped it onto Liam's back. He was still so small that he was easy to carry. They continued to water down the field and the building on the edge of the field where they put the caged animals. Then the wind picked up and embers blew about setting fire to the back of the field. Liam and Ken struggled to put out the new fire, but it got ahead of them. Still no fire trucks, but they could be heard in the distance.

Liam suddenly looked around at Ken and they both realized that they were almost surrounded. Thank heavens the fire was at the opposite end of where the caged animals were, but they were in serious trouble. Then they heard the whop, whop of the helicopter just settling down in the middle of the wet grass.

The pilot yelled "come aboard, you guys." He was a bit startled to see a small black bear on Liam's back.

"Wow, this is a first for me. Hold on tight." And he took off.

Liam and Ken echoed the pilot's comments. It was a first time for them too. Ken and Liam got credit for the quick response for the fire and an adventure they will never forget.

Saying Goodbye to Papa

By Dorothy Madden

My name is Emily Louise Lyons and I am 8 years old, or rather to be precise, I used to be 8 years old. I died two weeks ago and I think I am now a ghost and I don't know how ghosts figure ages. It was terrible for my mom and everyone, especially for my grandfather—my Papa—when I died. He didn't know that I died until three days ago because he was visiting his children in Germany and was camping in the mountains. He is on his way home now and that is why I am here. I am waiting to say goodbye to my Papa.

My Papa is the one I love the best. One of my earliest memories is his outstretched arms and his deep voice saying "Komm hier mein kleines maedchan," which means "Come to me my darling girl." When I ran to him, he would pick me up and swing me around, and when I hugged him tight I could smell his shaving cream.

When my father died, my mother moved into her old home with me and my brother Harry, who was a baby while I was two. But I knew that Papa loved me best and I think Grandma loved Harry best, so it worked out well for both of us.

Papa is the one who painted my room pink and helped me with my homework and taught me about the stars and planets and about beekeeping and making honey.

I stay in my room a lot because this is where he will come when he comes home to me, and also I don't really know where to go where no one is crying. I now know that no one can see me, but I try to make some sounds so they will know I am still here and every now and then I succeed, but they all come rushing upstairs only to find my room empty.

I have also discovered that there are certain people who can see me, well, not exactly see me, but what they believe is my spirit. One of these is Tante Marie, Papa's sister. One day I was on my bed when she came into my room and stopped dead. She looked at me and said, "Emily Louise, what are you still doing here?" I tried to speak and managed a garbled "I'm waiting for Papa."

"Oh, my darling girl," she said, and reached for me—but there was nothing to hold. I think that was the saddest time I have ever felt.

Then it occurred to me. What if Papa does not know me, and is not able to hold me? What would I do? Where would I go? Where do I belong? But all that became clear, for the next day Papa came home and came to my bedroom, as I knew he would. He looked at me and said "Komm hier mein kleines maedchan."

I went into his arms. He thanked me for waiting for him and told me that it was now necessary for me to move on to be with my father who is waiting in heaven for me and that he would see me soon. And so I did. I knew he would know exactly what to do. I am now in heaven—I guess that's where I am, for its beautiful and my father is with me.

A Simple Mistake

By Elvet Moore

My name is Forest Whittaker, and I'm a reporter working for the New York Daily News. I live by myself in a small apartment on the fifth floor of an old building on 45th street on the East side. Yesterday the mailman dropped off a letter addressed to me, and since I wasn't home when he came by, he placed it on the floor in front of my apartment door. When I arrived home I didn't initially see the letter, so I managed to step on it. When I picked it up I could see that I had badly smudged the return address, since I had some mud on the sole of one of my shoes.

Inside the envelope was a printed invitation to attend a party held by an organization calling themselves the *New York Roundtable Group (NYRG)*— an organization of persons who meet every week for breakfast at a deli on the corner of 45th and

Winchester. They sit together at a large roundtable capable of seating twenty persons comfortably, while they discuss the politics of the day. The invitation stated that the organization wished to expand its membership, and since I was in the newspaper business and lived nearby, my name was on their list of new member prospects.

Try as I might, I couldn't make out for sure the smudged return address. However I wrote down what I believed to be the address anyway—the corner of 95th and Winchester. So the next evening as I left my apartment to attend the party, I hailed a cab giving them the address I presumed to be correct, but which unbeknownst to me was forty blocks further away from the correct address.

The neighborhood where the taxi dropped me off was very dingy, with mostly rundown homes situated behind iron fences to prevent burglaries. Trash existed on the yards and porches, and on some steps a few old men were seated smoking and drinking beer. When I got out of the cab, they looked at me as if I was someone they wished would just go away and leave them alone.

I stood outside the gated entrance to 9510 Winchester, which was a very well kept recently painted and landscaped property, in the midst of the dingy surroundings. I asked one of the men sitting on the steps next door if this was the home of the NYRG organization. He just looked at me and frowned, without saying anything. The other men sitting with him also just frowned, but one of them said, "Why are you here, and what do you want with the NYRG organization?"

Ignoring him, I found the gated entrance not locked, so I opened the gate and walked up the sidewalk to the porch. When I got to the front door, someone from inside the house, who must have seen me arrive, opened the door. He was a man in his late 60's with long grey straggly hair that didn't look like it had been combed in years. He also sported a short beard and mustache, and wore faded jeans and a wool shirt which was not tucked in. His belly stuck out at least three inches, indicating that he had hoisted quite a few brews during his lifetime.

"I overheard you say something to Jim here that you were looking for the home of the NYRG organization. Is that correct?"

"Yes," I said. "I received an invitation to a party they are having tonight. Is that right?"

"Well, this is the home of the NYRG organization, but I know nothing about a party being held here tonight. Can I take a look at your invitation?"

The man took my invitation and studied it carefully. "Well, this certainly is an invitation to *an* NYRG organization, but not to *our* NYRG organization. Our organization stands for *New York Retired Guards,* whereas your invitation is for a party to be held by the *New York Roundtable Group.* How did you end up coming to this address?"

"The address on the invitation was smudged so I had to guess what it was. It's interesting though that this address is for an organization with the same last name. I'm a news reporter for the Daily News. Would you have some time if I were to come in and interview you to find out more about your organization?"

"Of course, come on in. We have fifteen residents living here now, who were once guards working for the city of New York. If you don't mind I'll have them all join us in the parlor so you can talk to all of us."

I spent the next couple of hours talking to the men who were all in their 60's. They had two things in common—their careers had been as guards assigned to the many public buildings and parks in New York City, and the second was that they had either never married or were widowers, and needed a place now to live with friends with common interests after they retired.

I gathered lots of information which I was able to include in a special report I published in the following week's paper. Because of that report, numerous retired guards who hadn't yet heard about the NYRG came forward to be interviewed. I guess my little mistake had taken on a purpose, for so many of the men had been looking for such an organization.

A Tropical Honeymoon

By Elvet Moore

My name is Julie Smith, and I am a single mom with a teenage daughter named Sally. I think I'm a reasonable mom, who lets her daughter have her own life, as long as she doesn't annoy others and as long as she gets herself ready to live a prosperous life. Today, however, I am really worried about Sally, for she has just turned 18 and she is determined to get married with a guy who I am not sure I care for.

"Sally, is that you?" I asked when the door opened, while I was getting the dinner food ready to eat.

"Yes, mom, it is I. I also have John Paul with me. Would it be okay if he and I ate here tonight before going to the movies?"

"As long as you clean up after you finish," I said.

"That's okay with both of us. Isn't that right, honey?"

"Sure, babe, let's first eat and then we'll split."

John Paul and Sally filled their plates with the beef stew I had prepared, and both of them sat down at the far end of the table where they could talk, but not so loud so I couldn't hear everything they had to say. When they finished eating they cleaned their plates and told me they were going to the theater downtown, and should be back around 10:00 pm.

This left me alone as I had found myself most evenings lately. I wondered if the relationship between Sally and John Paul was a good one. Even if it was, the thought of Sally getting hitched at such an early age caused me to become really worried.

About 10:15 pm the door opened and Sally entered by herself. She had said good night to John Paul in his car before coming home. What I did not know was that saying good night in John's car usually left her trembling all over, for he was all over her with both hands, and she wasn't sure if she knew how to shut him down or not.

"Sally, before you go to bed, can we talk in the living room," I said.

"Sure, mom, just as soon as I get out of these clothes and put on a pair of summer pajamas," she replied.

In a few moments Sally entered the living room and sat on the couch to my right. "Ok, mom, I'm here. What do you want to speak to me about?"

"Sally, I understand you want to get married in another month or so and then you and John Paul plan to go to the island of Maui in Hawaii for a nice honeymoon vacation. Is that right?"

"Yes, that's what we want to do. John Paul and I have been spending a lot of time talking about it, and we think a honeymoon like that would be a real nice way to start things off for us. It will cost a bit more than we had budgeted, but we think it's worth it. John Paul and I have been saving our money so we can handle the whole thing ourselves."

"Well, Sally, you must realize that this whole thing has hit me really hard. I hope you realize that your father and I never had the money to take such an exhaustive honeymoon. In fact, if he hadn't died recently, we would have probably done that just about now, not when we first got married. Are you sure you can afford such a lavish trip in such a short time?"

"Mom, don't you see what you did wrong? Back when you were married, you should have taken such a trip, for since you didn't, you really missed out on having lots of fun, even if it did cost you a lot. Anyway, John Paul and I will have saved enough money to make the trip work out for the both of us."

Time passed, and it was now the morning before the big wedding. John Paul had planned the affair to include only a hand full of their best friends, a fact that hadn't really pleased Sally that much, but she went along with it. She also hadn't worked out the Maui details very closely with John Paul, because he kept telling her that he wanted to surprise her with the details of the planned honeymoon.

After the wedding ceremony, Sally and John Paul arranged their clothes and other supplies. She went to her home and John went to his. In about two hours, they both met together at the local airport, each with a large suitcase. John Paul had the tickets, so he marched up to the counter and plunked them down. After checking their belongings, the couple boarded a

Boeing 737 which was headed for the Hawaiian Islands.

On board the plane, Sally seemed irritable, so John Paul asked her what the matter was. Well, it turned out that John Paul had used a lot of their budgeted money to obtain the tickets, since they found themselves seated in the first class section. He told Sally that it would be okay, and that they would just have to cut down on some of the other items of their trip to make up for the added cost. Meanwhile, he told her that they should enjoy the finer cuisine that came with the first class fare.

When they landed they were met by a Cadillac open air convertible, which John Paul had paid for to take them to their hotel suite, rather than having them wait for a bus full of hot and sweaty persons heading for the same part of town. Sally thought this was really nice, but she asked John Paul how much more it had cost. He told her to shut up and not to keep worrying about the money they were spending. "Let's just enjoy things," John Paul kept saying, so Sally decided to shut up and keep her concerns to herself.

When they entered the hotel, they were met by a couple of the staff who told them they had the honeymoon suite ready. After walking down the hall they opened the tall door at the end and found a wonderful room full of sample drinks and snacks and a perfect view of the ocean nearby. When they were left alone, Sally turned to John Paul and asked him again, what did this fancy room cost them?

"Sally, if you must know, he said belligerently, this honeymoon room costs us over $500 a day, compared with the $150 a day for the regular room downstairs, but it's worth it, don't you think?"

"But, John Paul, the cost of this room will blow our budget long before we are ready to return to the states," she said. "How are we supposed to enjoy this trip and have enough money left to return home?"

"Damn you Sally. Why do you always have to think of money? If we don't have enough, we'll contact your mother and ask her for more. I'm sure that will be okay with her, for after all what choice does she have? She wants us to be happy, doesn't she?"

The rest of the week continued the same way, with John Paul spending way more money that they didn't have on every kind of activity, party, or special meal. Sally had given up watching the costs accumulate; for she knew it would be a real issue, when they had to pay for everything.

The couple's tropical vacation had been ruined, for each and everything she had hoped for had been turned over by John Paul to be just one more item that cost more than the couple had to spend. When the day of reckoning arrived, and the couple had to pay for everything with their credit cards, the amount of money on credit was way over their maximum, so they had to contact her mother for the rest. It would take months, if not a year, for the couple and family to catch up to their excessive costs.

Back home, Julie was able to pound some sense into Sally, who finally realized that John Paul was not to be trusted, so she arranged for a quiet and very private divorce, which he and she gladly accepted. He had hoped for Sally to enjoy the lavish life style afforded her in Hawaii, but found it not to be, for everything he had planned for in his Tropical Paradise had gone south.

My Secret Room

By Elvet Moore

My name is Andrew Saltus, and my friends all call me Andy. Tomorrow is my birthday, and I will then become a more independent dude—in fact, I will become a man, for I will be 21—hooray!

My parents have never seemed to be very interested in what I do, as long as I don't get into serious trouble and keep my grades up to a C-average. Some of my friends think I've got it made, for all I hear from them is how their parents keep hassling them, trying to find out each and every detail of what they do with their lives—clearly not trusting them very much, that's for sure.

You need to be aware that I'm not all sweetness and lace, however. I sometimes hang out with some of the more aggressive of my school mates—those who are always trying to make out with some of the more flirtatious girls, or who are always playing dirty tricks in the classroom, when the teacher looks the other way.

It is this darker side of me that caused me to discover a room in the attic of our old Victorian home in downtown San Jose. I call this room my Secret Room and I often use it to catch cat naps on an inflatable mattress, or to sip club soda mixed with Irish whiskey. I once considered smoking weed, but I hate the smell of it, and the tell tail smell gives away the fact that someone is occupying the room, anyway.

Now that I am 21 I decided it's time I seriously consider losing my virginity, so last week I purchased a small cot and set it up in my Secret Room. I can now sleep with someone else in my bed. Now all I have to do is convince some sweet young thing to join me in my quest to become a man.

It's now seven o'clock in the evening and I decided to go to the bar at the corner of my street to see if I could pick up a girl. I also wanted to prove my manhood, for now at age 21, the barkeeper will let me drink almost anything.

"Hello, my name is Andy, and I turned 21 today so I can drink anything. Would you like for me to order you something?"

"Fellow, go sit down in the corner and leave me alone. I'm waiting here for a real man to pick me up. I'm not interested in having a pimple faced teenager like you try to make out with me."

Andy was shocked. He thought he was good looking enough to appeal to these experienced girls sitting at the bar, but they all disgustingly looked on while she berated him and it made him feel like two cents.

A younger girl then entered the bar and sat down near Andy. She seemed to be too young to buy drinks, so he figured that his original line might work. He tried it again.

"Hello, my name is Andy, and I turned 21 today and I can drink anything. Would you like for me to order you something?"

"Oh my yes, she said. My name is Gloria, and I have a fake ID card, for my real age is 16. Would you like to order me a Vodka Collins, and perhaps get one for yourself?"

Andy was ecstatic, for he had made his first score. After the drinks arrived, he asked Gloria to sit at a table with him where they could talk more openly about things. Andy bragged about his secret room, acting like it was a place he brought multiple women to make love, and Gloria began to believe him, as the cool contents of her drink slid down her throat. One thing led to another until the two of them left the bar, heading for Andy's secret room.

Unbeknownst to the both of them, a private Investigator was following them. His name was Gerald Holmes, employed by Gloria's father, who had found out that after his wife died, his sweet young daughter was all mixed up socially and was allegedly seducing boys from her school. As Andy and Gloria climbed the back stairs leading to his secret room, Gerald quietly followed them. He immediately opened the door, and broke up the love making before it had gone very far. He told Andy to beat it, and he took Gloria home with him to confront her father.

It's now several months later and Andy has not yet been successful in luring any girl into his secret room. Also, his parents had just put the place up for sale, so it would not be a secret for very much longer. On his way home one night walking along the waterway in his town, he spotted a girl on a raft, but that's another story.

Who Should I Meet

By Elvet Moore

If I should meet anyone it would be Thomas Alva Edison, for it was he who invented the electric light bulb. I wonder what he would be working on today if he were to re-appear on today's scene.

He had to try out various elements to use as filaments in his experimental bulbs and early on came to realize that the bulbs had to be totally without oxygen in them, for if they were not sealed, the filaments would catch fire and burn up, rather than glow as required in their application.

I would sit down with him and chastise him for being so stubborn when he first tried to connect a number of his bulbs together to wire a home for electric lighting. He was convinced that such a network had to use direct current electricity, rather than alternating current, which is the method of

155

choice today. Wiring up an individual home or apartment with direct current worked ok, but transmitting direct current electricity in a network from home to home would prove to be totally not practical.

If it weren't for an engineer in a company started by George Westinghouse, who suggested using alternate current, which could be increased or decreased through the use of transformers, electric lights in a large network like a city or country would have never happened.

So, why would I like to meet him, for won't he be so far removed technically from today's challenges that wouldn't it be a boring meeting. Perhaps so, but I would love to see how someone with his inherent smarts and tenacity would attack some of today's challenges. I have a feeling that after he listens to today's scientists about problems they consider important to work on, he would probably join forces with some team working on the cure for cancer, using some form of yet to be invented electrical procedure to kill cancer cells in the body without harming healthy tissue.

The Worst Decision

By Elvet Moore

The worst decision I have made is voting for
Donald Trump. I voted for him for two reasons. First I
didn't like the casual way Hillary acted about
securing classified information. She was sloppy and
didn't seem to care. Second I didn't know a lot about
Trump, but he seemed to be like a man I once worked
for at RCA, named Dr. Watters, who was able to force
the old line RCA bureaucracy to get things done.

He was hired from Polaroid Corporation to head
up the RCA Applied Research Division, and I think
the Bureaucrats in the RCA Departments never
seemed to ever get things done, so maybe a little
shaking up was warranted.

When video tape players were becoming available,
the RCA record division tried to enter that market
with 12" video records from the record division,

played on magnetic coated records with a player that looked like a conventional record player with needles and arms. Dr. Watters went behind the back of the record division and made a deal to buy JVC video tape machines from Japan and brand them RCA. This obviously pissed off the record division, but turned out to be the right thing for RCA to do.

To pacify the tube division, which needed more business, RCA TV sets using vacuum tubes continued to be built, even though competition began to use solid state components. Dr. Watters made deal with a French manufacture of TV that used solid state devices and had whole system boards sent to RCA to be repackaged into RCA sets. Right decision, but again embarrassed the old line group in charge.

The Tube division finally went *down the tubes* but that was inevitable anyway. Ultimately Dr. Watters got fired, and he went off the deep end, like Trump will do when he gets sacked next year.

Personal traits between Dr. Watters and Trump were similar—both womanizers, both pushed the boundaries of ethical behavior, both insulted people they thought to be inferior, etc. However, Watters had a good grasp of proper technical matters, while

158

unfortunately Trump seems to have virtually no grasp of anything but himself, so I definitely made a serious mistake and hope Article 25 of our Constitution corrects that error.

The Lonely Ghost

By Elvet Moore

In the town of Charlottesville, South Carolina, there stood an old homestead that had been there for several decades and which was the oldest property in the town. It had been over twenty years since anyone had occupied the home, so it didn't take long for the town's people to soon believe that there was an old ghost occupying the home, even though none had ever been seen, yet.

Inside the home there was the usual old furniture with webs of white dust connected from every arm or leg. Twenty years ago when the last person occupied the home, the owner caught a bit of the flu and ended up going to the town doctor, who placed him into a rest home under quarantine. Soon thereafter he passed away, and ever since then the old home has been empty, with the local bank holding the paper on it, hoping someone would come forward to want to live in the home. With the above as a background, I began my journey into living in the old city of Charlottesville, along with a ghost or two.

My name is Charles Swanson, and I am now 70 years old. My wife passed away last year, and we do not have any children, so I found myself very lonely. I soon found out that there was a city in the USA that offered a home to be managed and fixed up from scratch, so I decided to go there and take a good look at the old homestead myself. It was located in the outskirts of Charlottesville, South Carolina, USA.

When I arrived in the city, I proceeded directly to the bank where I found out details about 567 north Plains Boulevard, which had been empty for about twenty years.

The price for the home was about half the price of other homes of that age, which had not sunk into such a deep state of repair, so the obvious deal was to buy the home and spend a number of years fixing it up before selling it again, if I wanted to do so. Since I was alone and was lonely, it seemed to me that working on this home would be just what I needed to do in order to find a more relaxed state of mind for myself.

The bank mortgage fellow was very pleased to show me the home. Together we parked in front of it. The yard around the home had been kept up, so the home seemed to be okay, but beyond the grass and shrubs was a home that needed a lot fixing up for sure. The wood was rotten, and the paint was chipped off from what was left of the wood siding.

"Mr. Swanson, let's go into the home through the door on the right hand side of the porch," the mortgage fellow said, for he knew the front door was loose on its hinges.

"That's fine with me," I said.

In a couple of minutes we were both inside. Aside from the obvious white dust stretching from furniture arm to furniture leg, the home seemed to be carefully laid out. The furniture was a rather nice mixture of dark oak and light brown trim, so I figured it wouldn't take me long to get the house fixed up to look like something.

There was a second and third floor, and there was nice furniture at each landing and in each room. After spending a couple of hours I followed the mortgage fellow to the basement, where it appeared there would be only a black hole dug into the dirt. An old furnace was still there, and it looked like it hadn't been operated for several years.

After spending a number of hours examining the home, the mortgage fellow and I went back to his office and sat down to negotiate the price. On the market it was listed as $98K, which was about half the price for similar homes. I decided I could offer a bit less, however, since no one had wanted the home for all of these years. Hence, after much haggling I walked away with a price of $89K, and I was able to pay cash. I now owned the old home, and as soon as I fixed up the upstairs bedroom, I would have a place to hang my hat and other laundry items.

While fixing up the old place, I stayed in the town motel. It took me four weeks to fix things up, so afterwards I moved into the bedroom at the top of the stairs, and I was now in my own home sweet home.

In the meanwhile, there was an old friendly ghost living in the home. He usually stayed in the basement; for the darkness there afforded him the opportunity to sleep when he wanted to, or just hang out and read some material he had that was bright enough for him to see.

The ghost recognized my work to be aimed at fixing up the home and realized that in time he would have to come out of the basement and seek a better life living near me. He did not plan to scare me, however. He just wanted a friend like me to be with him whenever he sought friendship.

One night when I went to bed in the old bed upstairs, I was awakened by the sound of someone or something walking around the home. I quickly got out of bed and put on my slippers and walked down the stairs. To my surprise the old ghost was sitting in one of the large chairs in the living room reading his book.

He looked up and said to me, "Hello, I am living here, and I don't plan to scare you. Where are you living?"

"I usually hang out in the old bedroom at the head of the stairs. Have you been watching me all of this time while I fixed up the house?"

"I do get to see everything, but I didn't have any plan to scare you. Yes, I watched you, but I kept in the background."

The old ghost sat on the edge of my bed and fascinated me with the tales he told me. He had been

165

born an ordinary person in 1800, and having died a horrible death in 1820, he decided to play ghost ever since.

I asked him how is it that some persons who die end up being a ghost while others don't act ghostlike at all. He wasn't sure, but he said that he knew some ghost friends who could probably discuss the matter with a bit of reality, so he planned to take me to where they were.

After spending a few more weeks fixing up the home I found myself living in all the rooms with my ghost friend, who watched me, but who didn't bother me. Some other ghosts arrived in the basement of the home, but when we wanted them to leave they were willing to go immediately, so they jumped ship and didn't try to scare anyone.

I am now over 90 years old and I definitely do believe in ghosts. I wondered however if that would be the case if the ghosts in the old home had been the scary kind.

A Scary Sight

By Chuck Northup

The path was well-used, winding through the lush forest with hills and immense boulders all around. I just turned the corner past a big rock, and what I saw made my heart stop.

I'm the type of guy who likes to live in seclusion, so I moved to Montana where the population is low, and houses are far apart. To answer your questions, ladies, no, I'm not married, however I'm still trying to find someone who enjoys the great outdoors as much as I do and who doesn't care to go to parties and dances all the time.

My home is a comfortable two-bedroom place with a nice kitchen—yes, I like to cook, but I can give that up for the right lady—with plenty of land surrounding it for gardening or whatever. The place is located near Yellowstone National Park in a dingy little village called Bear Creek. The population is still small, so I'm not sure it qualifies as a village.

Mostly we have plenty of wildlife and good fishing. My home is rustic, but not crude. It was built by professionals, so everything really works—and it's up to date. It is in the Rocky Mountains, so there's lots of outdoors surrounding it.

We don't have the frivolities of big cities or even small towns, so we have to enjoy ourselves in more solitary pursuits, such as reading, hiking, fishing, photography, and other lonely hobbies. I do all of those things as well as cooking (You should taste what I can do with trout). My pasttime favorite, however, is hiking.

I usually take my camera along for the time that I see a good view, and I also carry a walking staff. You never know when you might see a rattler, and a staff is a fine weapon for reptiles. I normally don't go very far, but I can often hike for about five miles or so—but who's counting?"

This day I hiked along the creek. The snow melt had made it run pretty fast so there were lots of rapids. I thought they would make good photo shots with the water coming heavily over the rocks and splashing with foam. Trees in the background were more than green at this time.

Spring had sprung and all the needles on the pines were glistening, while the leaves on the hardwoods were in new growth. I wondered if I should have come back tomorrow with a fishing pole to pick up a line of trout for dinner. I just knew they were in those rapids waiting for me to show them a fly. They never see the hook, and by the time they bite, it's too late and they become dinner for me.

I've always known that Bear Creek got its name because of the many bears that come down for water and berries. Every now and then I would see a bear— usually a small black one, but most of the time they would stay clear of humans. They are more scared of us that we are of them. If they hear us coming, they usually disappear.

Today, however, was a very scary one. As I said, I had just rounded a big boulder, and my heart stood still. There before me was a grizzly, the biggest bear in the US. There are plenty of them in this area, but they are seldom ever seen. They don't like humans so they hide when we come around, if they hear us.

But today I was treading lightly. I wasn't singing or whistling, as the Rangers tell us to do when hiking, and I was alone—another thing they warn us about. The whole idea is to let the bears know you are there by making some noise or being in a group to seem like you are larger. Bears don't like anything bigger than they are.

Keep in mind that bears are mostly vegetarians, but they do eat meat like smaller animals or fish or garbage. The nearby park attracts more bears because of the garbage and the handy food they contain. Not all the bears pass into the park—most of them are still in the nearby Rockies.

I have read the notices put out by the Rangers about how to act when a bear is sighted. First, stand still, don't scream or run. If you run, the bear may go after you, and you cannot outrun a bear. They can run faster than a race horse.

Determine what the bear is doing. It may be eating something, drinking water, or just walking alone. Try not to look directly into its eyes, because that could be assumed to be a challenge. Turn and walk slowly away in the way you came. Be sure the bear has a way out of its position. Often you must walk sideways to allow the bear an escape route.

Make sure the bear knows you are a human by talking in a low tone and moving your arms slowly. Remember, they don't like humans. If the bear seems to attack, stand your ground by taking a step forward. Most bears will feign an attack, will growl or drool, or will show their teeth to intimidate the opponent. It may stand on its hind legs, but that is usually only to get a better look. You must make yourself larger by standing on a rock or raising your hand and staring into its eyes. These actions will usually scare the bear into leaving.

If the bear still attacks anyway, it is trouble time! Now is the moment for the walking staff to be put to use. Aim for the snout. Fight for your life. The bear doesn't have much desire to eat you, but if it bites it can cause great harm. Rolling into a ball might avoid injury. Playing dead usually doesn't help, but sometimes it can.

This day I simply stood still, raised my arms and staff, talked in a menacing way, and the bear turned and walked away. I was fortunate.

If this sort of encounter doesn't worry you, I'm still looking for the right lady to join me in this beautiful part of the world. Just write me at General Delivery, Havre, Montana, 59601.

A Spiriting Adventure

By Chuck Northup

I died a long time ago. I don't know how long because time doesn't exist where I am. I found myself in my old home where I lived for over sixty years. There are new people living in my old surroundings, and they get in the way.

I like to go back and walk the stairways and bedrooms I used to love. Sometimes the people wake up when I'm there, and they think they see me. Maybe they can—perhaps they can because they seem to get scared. I'm not sure what they are scared about—I won't hurt them. I just like to be back home once in a while.

One time I was at the foot of the stairway, and a woman came out of the kitchen and saw me standing there. She seemed puzzled so I raised my hands over my head. I attempted to say something, but all that came out was "Whooo." I guess speaking is not possible in my state.

Young people don't seem so afraid. Kids just look at me and usually tell their mother they saw a ghost. Their mother usually tells them that they were dreaming, and the whole thing goes away.

I don't know where my wife is, or she would probably join me. Sometimes I find another spirit (that's what we're called), and we go together, and I show them my old home.

We often scare the living people just for the fun of it. We don't have to worry about doors or walls—we can go right through them, so we have easy access to any place we want.

Travel is easy also. We simply think of where we want to be, and we are immediately transported to that place.

I keep saying, "We", because there are many of us spirits here. I can't tell you where here is, for I don't know myself. We seem to be in a waiting room of sorts, on our way to another place.

Other spirits have already proceeded to that other place, but we in the waiting room must just hang around somewhere between, but be earth bound. It's boring, so we go to places in old homes just to have something to do.

There is a place in San Jose that we use as a club. A lot of us join together to visit the club and we have fun. Lots of living people come just to see us or hear about us. We like to give them a good show for their money, so we make noises and howl and bring chains to rattle. Its good fun to scare people who pay for it (too bad we don't get to keep the money). There are lots of clubs around the world. I've even been inside castles.

The sponsors of those "haunted houses" claim that we are the ghosts of past kings, queens, or other noblemen, but really we are more recent. Those spirits have long passed on to that other place. I've been to so many countries. It doesn't matter what language is spoken since we don't speak. We simply think, and other spirits seem to understand us. Most people think we are dressed in a shroud or sheet with holes cut out to look through. That's bad thinking. We are dressed in the clothes we died in. A good share of us died in bed in a hospital, so our clothing is just one of those nightgowns with an open back.

By the way, we don't need holes in a sheet to see through—we can see through anything. In addition, we can make things move by simply thinking about it. We don't have to pick up anything—we can't anyway. Those chains I mentioned are only props left around for us to play with, just like your kids have blocks to play with.

Well, I must go now—another spirit just invited me to go to Australia to see what it is like there. I've never been there so I am looking forward to the trip. It takes no time at all—we just think of it together, and there we are. So, until I haunt you again, G'day Mate.

Future Planning

By Chuck Northup

Kevin had finished college with an Accounting major, and he had found a good job with a CPA firm locally. During his last year in school he dated Jenny, a very tall Scandinavian blonde with a statuesque body. Kevin had dated many girls while in college, but none of them could put up with his conservative mind—the kind that analyzes things carefully, as good accountants tend to do.

As an example, he was always careful when eating out that the tax and tip were perfectly figured. His clothing also reflected his conservative views—some would call him cheap—when he went shopping. He was always conscious about money, and most women didn't like that when dating, for they eventually would say something that turned him off.

When he met Jenny, however, it was a different story. She actually enjoyed his way of doing things inexpensively. She liked a man who could actually save money toward the future. She took that into account when they reached the point of dating exclusively, because she looked forward to spending a whole lot of her life with him.

"Why don't we get married," she said one day.

"I'd like that, but we should wait until my job is really secure," he answered.

This sort of conversation kept going on for several months. They finally began living together. She had procured a job as an Occupational Therapist with a nearby hospital, so there were now two incomes. Between them they had saved enough money to put a good down payment on a home.

One day she went to see her doctor, because she had missed her period and she wanted to be tested for pregnancy. The doctor sent the test to a lab and told her she would get the results in the mail in a couple of days. She had said nothing to Kevin about the doctor visit or the test or the missed period. She eagerly awaited the letter, and when it finally came she was home alone. The news was positive.

That evening when Kevin arrived, she had dressed in a demure outfit and caught Kevin as he came in the front door.

He said, "What's the occasion?"

She said, "I didn't feel like cooking tonight. Let's eat out."

"OK, that sounds good to me, too. Got any place in mind?"

"I'd like to go to Henri's. It's nice and romantic."

"Keven said, "That's a pretty expensive spot. Are you sure you'd like to go there."

"Yes, but I'm going to eat light tonight anyway, so the bill won't be very high."

"OK, but wait till I change into something better looking," Kevin said.

The evening went smoothly. Jenny ate only an appetizer and declined any wine. Finally, she broke the mood by saying, "I want to get married. We have enough money saved now, and your job seems like it will last, and so will mine."

He answered, "I agree. Let's set the date."

She was overjoyed by his willingness, so she followed up the BIG announcement. "I'm pregnant," she said.

"You are? How do you know?"

"I got the test results today—I didn't want to tell you in the kitchen."

He said, "I'm really happy for us!"

"Let's move into our new home before the baby comes. We still have several months to get furniture and settle in," she said.

"That sounds like a good plan to me. I'll talk to the realtor tomorrow to see if she can put everything together right away."

He paid the bill and they went home. When the lights were out, and she had snuggled up to him in bed, she said, "This is your entire fault."

He said, "I hope so."

Lunch with Sam

By Chuck Northup

I have worked in the same office with Sam for several years, but only recently did I have such an intimate discussion with him. I often have lunch with Sam, and we talk about most everything, but this time the subject of homosexuality came up. I had an idea that Sam might be gay, but it wasn't sure and it didn't bother me.

Sam said, "When I was out with Paul the other night, we were detained by the police, questioned, and allowed to leave. It was scary."

I asked, "Why did they stop you?"

We were in a place that's well-known as a gay hang out, but we were not doing anything that would cause an arrest, so we were released."

"That is really pretty scary. Do you hang out at places like that often?"

"Well, not often, but sometimes. You know I'm gay, don't you?"

"Well, I thought you could be, but the subject never came up. When did you realize you might be gay?"

"I didn't know for sure until I was about twelve. Before that the kids called me a name and wouldn't play with me. It was pretty lonely, but later on, when I got more knowledge, I realized I was not like other boys, so I figured I must be gay. As I got into adolescence, it became clear that I didn't enjoy girls like other guys did."

I asked, "Do you mean you weren't talked into it by someone older? That's what I've always heard."

"No, that might happen sometimes, but not with me. I just was born with those feelings. I guess my hormones decided what I am. By the time I was fourteen, I knew I liked boys, and liked other guys too, so I became active sexually."

"Without being descriptive, what do you mean active?"

"It started when I was dating, just like anyone else. You find some guy you like, and you go out on a date. You soon find out how far things go."

182

"I guess dating is about the same as between straight men and women, except we don't get arrested for being together."

"Yeah, that's a big problem. We are discriminated against all the time just for being ourselves. Most of the public doesn't like us, and the police take action against us when they haven't much else to do. It's been that way for generations."

"I imagine it's like being black and getting arrested for little reason—like for being in the wrong place."

"Yeah, that happens a lot. I've been lucky and never got arrested or taken to jail. That would be really bad. The things that happen to gays in jail get very serious—even deadly. They are usually raped by several men and then beaten badly."

"When that kind of arrest occurs, a gay is forced out, so everyone knows. Is that right?"

"Probably, but if it stays out of the papers, he may still not be outed."

"You've never made your gayness known as far as I know. Have you ever come out?"

"Well, my family knows, but I'm not completely out. It would not be wise in the business you and I are working. Our boss knows, but it is not broadcasted—

we might lose a lot of customers because of their prejudices. But in some lines of work, it doesn't seem to matter that much whether one is out or not. What's worst is being outed when one is trying to stay in the closet. That has devastating effects everywhere—especially if the person is famous."

"Well, I can imagine in some professions it would matter, such as teaching young children, scouting, or jobs like that."

Sam said, "Those are the obvious ones, but from my point of view there are many personnel directors who are homophobic and won't hire anyone gay—PERIOD. I see that all the time, so I hide my preferences in those situations.

I queried, "Doesn't that keep a lot of intelligent people out of the workforce?"

"Sure. Businesses don't know what they are missing. There are many talented people who fall into the LGBTQ category, but are ignored."

"Sam, you don't act gay or queer. Why do some people act or talk in a funny way?"

"That's just an affectation. It doesn't come naturally. They learned to act that way—they are just acting. They do that so most people will know they are gay, and they just don't care. They are in constant danger, however, from those who hate gays and who may attack them anytime.

I said, "That seems crazy—like they are asking for trouble."

"Most gays do not act that way. You seldom know who is gay. There are several in our office whom you don't even suspect. I know who they are but that's because I'm in the inner ring of knowledge. In our company of around eighty workers, there are at least eight gays—both men and women."

"Eight?! I thought you might be the only one, and I wasn't even sure about that. That's ten percent. Is that number normal?"

"Well, normal is a subjective word. Some psychologists say fifteen percent would be more accurate, but statistics show a bit over four percent claiming's correct, not counting those in the closet.

"You also have to consider others of a slightly different bent, such as the trans genders and cross dresses, as well as those who still don't know for sure what or who they are. There are also people well along in years who are still in doubt about their sexual preference."

"How do they live so long without knowing?"

"Who knows? They just don't seek counselling or don't ask the right people. You know most families do not talk about sex while their kids are young. It is a forbidden subject in most cases, so how is a kid supposed to find out about sex and its varieties? If he or she asks a friend, it would be too revealing, so they don't ask.

"Many times, they find out by dating. Sometimes they find out by introspection—and that is difficult. It's just not easy. But remember, about eighty percent of the people don't have this worry.

"Yeah, they just muddle along like I do—go out with girls, get married, find out what is good or bad, perhaps get divorced or married again, and so forth."

Sam said, "Gay folks do that too, except most of them do not marry. They just live with one another—split up—rejoin with someone else, etc., same as you said for straights."

"I guess we're all alike in that way. But you mentioned straights. A lot of straights get involved with gays, don't they?"

"They sure do. You begin to wonder about the figures psychologists use when counting the LGBTQ group. If you add in the straights who mingle with gays, the percentages get huge."

"But isn't that just a fling?"

"It may be, but why choose someone of the same sex? Why not fling with someone of the opposite sex? There must be something else going on in their brain. Are they questioning their sexuality? Keep in mind that it was accepted back in the Greek and Roman days, even with married men. That often took the form of pederasty."

"That's probably an unanswerable question. But with that still hanging in the air, let's pay our total bill and get out of here. I've had enough coffee for one night."

Mystery Address

By Chuck Northup

I live in Houston, TX. I'm still a bachelor, but I still enjoy parties—especially with women. I haven't reached forty yet, so I'm still interested. My day got brighter when I received a post card from an old girlfriend named Dolly. I had not seen her for several years. I remembered many good times and nights with her when she lived in Houston. She moved away to someplace far away, but I don't know where.

This card brought up all the great memories we shared about seven years ago. I wondered if she was the same really cute blonde Dolly I knew before, or if she had gotten fat and sloppy, or what.

It was only a card—not a letter. I'm not sure why she wrote that way, but the invitation was certainly sincere enough. It read:

"Hi, Jamie. Long time no see. It would sure be nice to have you close again. I'm having a little party on Saturday, August 5th and hoped you could find time to come. We won't get to buzzing until around nine at night, but you can count on a swell time. The address is—and here's where the postmark wrote right over the number—Cleveland Avenue, New Orleans. No RSVP needed. Just come—and I do mean YOU" It was simply signed Dolly.

There was no phone number so I looked up the address to try to find one, but there was none. I got a New Orleans phone directory and looked up her name, but came up with the same story—nothing.

New Orleans is about 350 miles away, and that's quite a trip. It's not far enough to fly and yet almost too far to drive, but I decided to use the car. Dolly said nothing about staying overnight so I had better get a room for the night—I knew well enough that I wouldn't be able to drive back after the party.

I checked with a street map of New Orleans because I hadn't been there but only once or twice, and didn't know the area at all. I found that Cleveland seemed somewhat like Bourbon Street, so I figured it was in a "hot spot." That would be just like Dolly.

The day finally arrived. I dressed down knowing Dolly wasn't for big dress up-affairs. I tossed an extra shirt and underwear into a small bag and hopped into the car. I gave myself plenty of time to get there, but I stopped off at the local liquor store and picked up what I remembered was Dolly's favorite booze— pomegranate-flavored vodka. I can't stand the stuff but she goes crazy over it, as I remember. With my bottle and map in hand, off I went.

I reached the city in about seven hours and found my hotel—a cheap one that seemed to be what I thought might be near my destination. I picked up a quick dinner—nothing fancy—and then started on my search for the unknown address.

Looking again at the post card I could make out four numerals in the address, and one of them was probably a three. The rest were all obliterated. The three was in the second position, so it was not much help.

I found that Cleveland was a very long avenue and nowhere near Bourbon Street. I drove to the very end of it and realized that the addresses at that point were three numerals long. That meant I had to be at the other end of the avenue, or at least about ten blocks further away.

Some of Cleveland had a school yard, and some of it had businesses but no houses. I got into a more residential area where there were plenty of homes, plus a few mom and pop stores on corners. This area was definitely not a "hot" spot, for there were no night clubs or restaurants. Blocks were quite short, and many had only the sides of homes—no fronts. I could discount them.

I got into the 3,000 block, and things looked more promising. The street had become narrow and one way. Cars were parked along both sides, leaving only one lane down the middle. I crept along looking for a house with a party. It was getting later and later so Dolly's party must be in full swing by now. I saw a house with lots of lights on, so I thought that it might be the one.

Parking was another problem. There was none. I drove about three more blocks and found a spot for my car. I got out and walked back to the house with all the lights, went up to the door, and rang. A really fat black woman opened the door a bit.

"What do you want, whitey?"

"I said, "Is Dolly there?"

She just slammed the door. I guess that wasn't the place.

I decided to ask at one of the corner markets where she may be recognized. On the way back to car, I stopped at Washateria, a small launderette on the corner. A couple of ladies were doing their laundry there, and I asked them if a lady named Dolly lived around here.

They were much nicer, and they even spoke to each other about the question. One lady said to me, "There's a blonde lady living down on Cleveland about two blocks. She lives in a two-story yellow house with a balcony. It's on the left side of the street. You might check there."

That was in the opposite direction of my car, but since I had a spot for parking, I figured I'd better walk on. The street was crowded with parked cars, and it was very dark. I had gone only a couple of hundred yards when a big man in a hoodie stepped out from between two houses and said, "Hey, Buddy, give me the bottle!"

He took me by surprise, and I realized that I was carrying the bottle in a sack just like any other street drunk. He was very intimidating and I couldn't make out his face. I won't know if he was white or black, since he was unshaven and the hoody shaded his face. I simply held out the bottle to him.

"Now give me your wallet!" he said gruffly." I dug into my jacket and handed him my billfold, stuffed with credit cards and other junk. He went right to the currency, took it all, ignored the credit cards, and threw my wallet onto the ground.

I stepped over to it and scooped it off the side walk. When I stood up straight again, I saw him going between buildings, while taking a swig out of my expensive vodka, still in the bag.

Shaken, I walked on to the yellow house another block or so beyond. It was an apartment house. The doorbell panel had several buttons with only numbers, so I put my finger on the first buzzer and waited. There were no lights or people to be seen. Soon an older lady opened the peek hole and spoke to me.

"What do you want?"

I told her I was looking for Dolly, and she told me, "Room 8."

Wow! I found her! I rang the room number and the door opener clicked. I went inside the hall, then upstairs. When I looked up the stairs, I saw her. There she was. She was so beautiful! Her arms were spread out to greet me. She had a dress that just barely covered her breasts and didn't reach her knees.

When I reached the top, she hugged me and grabbed my crotch.

"Dolly, slow down, we're still outside in the hall!"

We went into her room like Siamese twins, shut the door, and began kissing. When I came up for air, I asked, "Where is the party?"

She said, "You're it! I finally found a place to live, and I couldn't wait to see you."

I remarked, "Could we sit down? I'm shaken because I've just been mugged."

"That's usual around here," she said, "But just wait until I mug you, honey!"

I didn't expect a party like this. The bum got most of my booze and most of my money, but he didn't see the hidden compartment in my wallet or my credit cards, so I'm not totally broke. We can still have a great time together.

"Don't worry about spending money. I've got plenty of liquor, and we're not going anywhere," she said.

Well, as you can guess, I never used my hotel room that night.

The Bird Cage

By Chuck Northup

It is a cozy spot to have a drink. It caters to birds—and they are always thirsty. The specialty of the bar is Wild Turkey, and they sell plenty of it.

If you go in on a week night, the place is not terribly crowded, but it is still haven to plenty of birds who have nowhere else to spend time. After your eyes become accustomed to the dim lighting, you might see a gaggle of geese in the corner cubicle, or a murder of crows in the darkest booth.

On the weekends there is usually a warbler putting out her heart for the drinkers, and often there is a standup mockingbird doing mimicry with a laughing gull holding his sides in uproar. Invariably, on Friday nights, at the corner of the bar, is a group of very sad birds drinking themselves into a stupor—blue birds, blue herons, and blue jays—each with a sadder story to tell to make everyone feel worse than when they came in.

If the warbler gets going there is usually a chain of bobolinks bobbing around with a red, red robin bobbing along with them in the middle of the room. Occasionally, when the song sparrow isn't around they put on a loud group of screech owls for the modern music lovers. At his usual stool, an old bald eagle holds court, unbeknownst that right behind him a red bellied woodpecker is showing off his fat front to the giggling goose nearby.

Just then the phone rings, and Sharpy answers. "Yeah, Bird Cage—Sharpy here."

After listening a moment, he shouted, "Dr. Stork—it's for you."

The stork came over and standing on one leg, he said, "Stork here—what address?" Then he flew off to deliver a baby.

One weekend a trio walked in. It was a dove, a sparrow, and a PIG! The bartender spotted them immediately and shouted, "Get that fat pig outa' here—and fast! We don't allow four-footed cloven hoofed, unclean mammals in here."

"But Sharpy, he's a friend of ours. We've been together for years."

"Take your friend somewhere else. He's not welcome here," said the sharp shinned hawk bartender.

"Are you discriminating against him?" they asked.

"You bet I am. You two birds can stay if you want, but he's gotta' go."

Just then the parliament of owls in the second booth spoke up. "Let him stay. If they sue, you'll lose and won't have a bar anymore."

The venue of vultures agreed. "Yeah, let him stay."

Sharpy saw that he was outnumbered when a fall of woodcocks and an execution of larks joined into the argument. Sharpy relented and said, "OK, you can stay if you behave."

Now the Birdcage keeps a small pond in the corner to satisfy the mallards and other water fowl. The pig took one look at that pond and climbed in. A coot waitress came over and took his order—a Whistle Pig straight rye on the rocks. It wasn't long before the pond became a mud hole.

Sharpy was getting madder by the minute, but just then the cuckoo came out of the clock and cuckooed twice.

Sharpy shouted, "Closing time! Drink up! Get the flock out!"

The Clubhouse

By Chuck Northup

It seemed to take forever. My two sons, Joey-9 and Harold-11 were hauling boards, nails, tools, and canvas out to the river on the acreage nearby. It was an unused piece of land belonging to a friendly gent who didn't mine the boys tramping around on his property.

The area on which the boys did their scheming was in a grove of trees near the edge of the river. There were lots of overhanging branches they could play in, or they could just hang around in the bushes pretending they were Indians.

At this juncture they had decided to build a clubhouse. It would be a hideaway from adults—a spot where they would get privacy now that they were all grown up. In the summer they could lie beneath the trees and watch the wind rustle the leaves slightly. They could hear the murmuring of the snow-moving river as it went past. At times they would take fishing poles and bait to catch the local denizens who were unwary. Later they would build a campfire and cook the fish on the end of a stick. The burnt carcasses usually dropped into the fire and were seldom eaten, but it was fun just the same.

The boards they hauled in were to make a small framework of sorts with a canvas thrown over to provide shelter when the rains came. It took a long time to build. Cutting and nailing the boards to the right length required some simple strategy and planning, but when finished made quite a nice club house, even if it was a little bit crude.

Of course, they told their friends at school, and soon their clubhouse became a hangout for others. Some were lots older—even twelve or more, and they brought things that were not seen in Joey's or Harold's home. Some reading matter was just a bit salacious for younger boys, but they ate it up anyway.

One day, young Joey came home early because he wanted to work on his stamp collection. Some beautiful exciting new triangular stamps from Costa Rica had arrived in the mail, and he was anxious to see them and read about them. They needed placing into his album.

Harold had stayed behind by the river. Time passed and he had not come home. I became worried. Bad thoughts went through my head. Did he fall into the river? Was he hurt? He was always good about getting home on time, but tonight he was unusually late.

I decided to go looking for him. I had never seen their clubhouse, so I was also interested in observing what they had done. They had built their clubhouse on the banks of the river, hidden by reeds. It could hardly be called a building—it was more like a shanty, but for boys of their age, it was a castle. The reeds kept people from seeing them as they sailed by, and surrounding bushes kept out prying eyes. If I didn't know where to look, it would have escaped my discovery.

But there it was. I didn't wish to intrude on their privacy, so I called out, "Harold, are you OK?"

He called back, "Yes, Dad, I lost track of time."

I pulled back the canvas that served as a door, and Harold was busy hiding something under some magazines.

"What are you reading?" I asked.

"Some of the guys brought some new magazines, and I was looking at them," Harold muttered.

I reached into the stack of magazines he had hidden and found one he was reading. It was a girly magazine. It was not very revealing but did show plenty of skin. Looking at this type of photo was new to Harold, and I said without anger, "It looks like you are getting an interest in girls. That's about right for your age. I was your age when I found out about girls. But it's late, and your mother has dinner ready. Better come on home now."

Later that night after the boys had gone to bed, I told Mother about my experience at the clubhouse. I told her I will have a man-to-man talk with Harold tomorrow. She agreed that it was time to have "that talk" with Harold so he gets off on the right foot. It's also nice to know that he is not gay.

The Mistake

By Chuck Northup

My name is Solomon Fischer. Growing up, the kids used to call me salmon, so I finally shortened it to Sal. I was raised in Silicon Valley, and as a result grew up to learn and love all about space. I schooled normally, but in college I specialized in space exploration. When the time came to join the group headed for space in a space ship, I paid my money up front—not cheap—and after several years of waiting, finally had the lift to go around Mars and even land if possible.

This space capsule took a lot of preparation. The space capsule was well fitted to accept the number of people who were going. In our case it was only fourteen, chosen because of their talent, knowledge and expertise of what to do while in flight or longer— if we did actually get to land. The cabin was outfitted so that no one had to wear space suits while in flight. We could walk about and really float.

The interior of the capsule is roomy. In the past there was room for only seven astronauts, but modern improvements have enabled engineers to make much larger capsules. The monitors all may be folded away, the seats are very comfortable, and they have double use as beds. Food must still be eaten from bottles, since lack of gravity precludes open plates, cups, or bowls. Toileting is still a major problem, not easily solved, but with more space allowance there is a private area to accommodate this need, where one can do the necessary into a vacuum tube, which is then ejected into space. Temperature control has been solved, so all passengers are carried in comfort.

On the outside, the capsule is protected against heat buildup with heat-proof covering and the landing legs drop down in time for an easy landing on the spot. On our trip to Mars this event will not happen for eight to nine months, depending upon the orbit selected and where Mars is in relation to Earth. The planet reaches its closest point every seven years, but some travelers may take the trip at other times.

We got to know each other quite well—we were always together. Amazingly, there were no fights. We did have a few minor disagreements, however, but never any hurt feelings. All were very professional because everyone had a job to do, and we all depended on each other. Most of our time was spare time, and we spent it in reading and studying, but of course, we did a lot of sleeping. We had communication with Earth and with our families. We had to share these moments so all would have their chance to talk with friends, neighbors, and family.

Space control on Earth was always in control, but we had to respond to orders from time to time for minor corrections or to consider space junk flying too close. When landing time was imminent everyone sprang into action. We all had our duties at various monitors or instruments. We were in constant contact with space central at that time to tell them of conditions on the landing spot.

It is very touchy because space control cannot know the exact condition of the landing area. My job was to watch through the bottom portal for obstructions and notify the radioman who would convey my observations to space central. Others controlled the speed of descent with propulsion jets mounted in the lower portion of the capsule.

We had a very soft landing, fortunately, with no mishaps. No one had even landed in this part of Mars before, so we did not know what to expect. Prior landings had been further away, and the major task was to find water and set up living accommodations. There was never any report of living creatures where we were going.

We got into our space suits with helmets and breathing tanks. One person was in charge of opening the portal door and lowering the ladder so we could get out. I was not the first to exit. The poor soul who did set foot on Mars first was immediately enveloped by an alien being that appeared from the soil under our capsule. That alien being simply appeared from nowhere, grabbed the astronaut, and took him back into the soil it had come from. It was mostly out of my sight because I was still in the capsule and could barely see it. The alien being was gray and had some way to move about. To me it seemed like a blob of putty with no features. It could easily wrap around the astronaut since it was so large.

We will never know what happened to our crew man. We immediately closed the hatch and notified space control, and they informed us to take off as soon as we could, as our capsule is equipped for propelling us back into space at the proper speed to enable us to return to Earth. However, when we hit the switch to enable us, nothing happened. Space control should have been able to guide us again to a landing in the ocean so the capsule could be used again, but nothing happened. We were in effect caught between a rock and a hard place, for if we left the module, the alien being would grab us, and if we tried to take off again, nothing would happen.

My trip to Mars was exciting, adventurous, and filled with memories to tell my grandchildren, but the error that occurred on it created a very expensive mistake for the lost crewman and for the rest of us. We just sat on board the ship until the oxygen ran out, and from then on, we were in a permanent grave.

About a Grandfather

By Betty Stearns

As my readers know, my new friend, the little mourning cloak butter fly, continued to fly down from a Chinese Elm tree to sit by me for two or three times a day for three weeks—a long time for butter flies. Then an amazing thing happened—we began to really understand each other's speech.

Knowing I was to write a story about a grandfather, I asked her, "Do you have a grandfather?"

The little butter fly answered, "Yes, I do. He is very old—almost three years old by the way you calculate time."

I said, "That's almost 100 years old. My grandfather lived to be one hundred and 4."

"Wow," said the little butterfly. "What kept him so healthy? What did he eat? My grandfather ate tree sap, fruits, and sugars excreted from aphids."

I said," My grandfather ate a big bowl of oatmeal for breakfast and dry bread and peanut butter for lunch."

My grandfather was raised in Maine. At about age 20, he was told that he might get T.B. unless he moved to a warmer climate—so he came to California. He stopped in Kansas on the way and learned to conserve water—always taking dirty dish water out doors to water the plants.

He first worked as a Latin teacher and then as a Christian minister working mostly on horseback. He was very strong, walked everywhere, and kept the plants growing.

"Was your grandfather as strong, little butter fly?"

"Oh yes. He flew from very far away and even led a large migration of birds, but also he was quite a lady's man. Female butter flies gathered around him a lot. He ended up with quite a few wives. And did you know that we were chosen as the state insect of Montana?"

"I had never heard that! The only fact I can recall to bring us some fame is that Prince Street in Berkeley, California, was named after my great grandfather's favorite horse."

"Well, little Mourning Cloak butterfly, I have loved being your friend. I have loved talking with you—what a miracle!

"Rather than being *Mourning Cloak*, I can also be called *White Petticoat*, for it makes me feel younger!"

Mt. Fuji Climb

By Betty Stearns

Not far from Mt. Fuji in Japan was Ninooka, a beautiful little village where missionaries gathered in the summer for a well-earned rest. It was known that my father climbed Mt. Fuji almost every summer and offered to guide anyone who had reached a 12th birthday, and I was lucky to have reached 12 before we left Japan.

Our Mt. Fuji hike that year was so special for me, that I have always wanted to repeat the climb with my husband, Wally.

"Wally, how about it? We've talked about it, but let's really do it this year." He was agreeable, and soon we were having fun making serious plans together.

"Wally, there are many things I want us to experience—like each climber had a big wooden pole which was stamped at each little rest stop. And at each rest stop you were given a cup of green tea (so refreshing!) and then a "tatami" area where you could really stretch out."

I remember as we reached the 3rd or 4th rest stop station, there were little charcoal stoves to warm our hands.

"Wally, did I tell you that we walked all night in order to get to the top by sunrise. It was so quiet! Once in a while we would meet up with another climber."

We were awed by the billions of stars above us. Even at that age I was reminded of the psalm my mother had us all memorize:

> When I look at your heavens, the work of your fingers, the moon and the stars, which you have set in place, what is man that you are mindful of him, or the son of man that you care for him?

We were thrilled when we made it to the top by sunrise and felt quite emotional when we stood with about nineteen or twenty two Japanese who had hands clasped, and facing east, praying as the sun rose.

"Wally, can you believe it? We are actually beginning our Mt. Fuji climb. This metal ski pole will do ok, instead of those wonderful old wooden poles. Get your camera out—we will see the first stop as we turn at the next corner."

"Oh, my soul! Oh No! I don't believe it. I see the golden arches of MacDonalds, and a group of noisy teenagers pigging out on hamburgers!"

Climbing further we encounter a young man handing out coupons for a special sale at Walmarts, station 5. Oh! No! Not Walmarts!! Unbelievable!!

As we approach the final turn before the summit, we are sucked into a huge crowd kept together by ropes (as in Disney land) each pushing ahead to make it to the top to see the sunrise. "Wally, I'm trying to hang on, but this is a stampede!"

"Wally, don't let go of me!! Oh No!! You are disappearing!! Wally!!"

"Betty, you are talking in your sleep again. Were you having a bad dream?"

"I don't recall but I have a strong feeling that we should complete our plans VERY SOON before any more changes are made on this sacred mountain."

The "dream idea" came to my mind after seeing in the Smithsonian's a recent photograph of huge crowds of tourists pushing up toward the summit of Mt. Fuji.

My Six Word Story

By Betty Stearns

At Westminster House, just across the street from UC Berkeley, an enthusiastic group of college students were gathered to sing hymns and World War II songs. My sister Ernestine was one of them. She looked at her watch and jumped up, hurrying to the door. Being a student nurse, she had to obey the Merritt Hospital curfew.

She ran down to Telegraph Avenue where the street car stopped. As she stepped onto the street car, a young man followed and sat down directly behind her. Then as she got off at the Merritt stop, she noticed that he pulled the chain to get off at the next stop.

She hurried to the pathway leading up to the little hill at the back door of the hospital where student nurses could slip in. About half way up the path, she heard footsteps edged toward the right and looked up to see a hatchet aimed at her head.

Fortunately, her roommate was saying good night to her boyfriend, and seeing blood pouring down Ernestine's head and neck, she immediately called doctors for help.

Within minutes her hospital bed was surrounded by reporters with cameras and questions. She arose to the occasion with fresh bright lipstick, big smile, and neatly combed hair showing below her bandages.

The next day before I, being on the elevator of the American Trust Company in S.F. where I worked, surrounded by workers earnestly looking at the latest headlines, could not help but say importantly, I am the sister of that nurse.

Some new facts were uncovered, with more headlines appearing for weeks:

Nurse Hacked by Powler on Hospital grounds.
Youth, 17 years old, held for attack on student nurse.
Youth nabbed in beauty assault.
Oakland Nurse to face hatcher attacker.
Nurse taken to Ukiah to possibly identify attacker.
Nurse identifies Hatcher.

There is always a silver lining. A telegram arrived from her boyfriend camping in the beautiful Sierras which said, "I always said you would make the headlines. Probably get a movie contract out of that."

The Three Poor Souls

By Betty Stearns

I have thought, "If we can put a man on the moon we should be able to invent nylons that don't run and easily provide for the many street people we see every day. It's not that complicated. I drive past them and I feel guilty for the next few minutes at least.

The opportunity came when I was told that a delicious dinner would be delivered to my house, and all I had to do was invite three guests. At least I could do my part and provide a good meal for three poor souls.

The three I invited were Mary, John, and Bob, for I see them quite often. Mary sits on the cement with two little children, just outside the big post office— John is often at the exit of the big Safeway parking lot—and Bob sits on the wall just outside the liquor store nearby.

When I welcomed them to my small cozy dining room, I was pleased to find out how friendly all three were. I asked Mary, "Were you able to get a baby sister for your two little children?"

Mary replied, "You have been so kind to invite me. I want to tell you my secret. The two are not my children. I borrowed them to make me look needier. I have worked very hard looking for a job and finally found one, so now I want to begin to save a little each week toward a home of my own. If this fact were known, my earnings might be gone.

"John, how about you? You began to show up at the Safeway area only a month ago. Where did you come from?"

"I came from the other side of the city where we lived, so my friends would not see my humiliation. A year ago we were able to open a small restaurant. We were thrilled at how popular we had become.

"We even planned our first ever vacation to Hawaii. Then the notice came saying that our lease was going to double. With that increase, there was no way we could pay our three waiters, the gas, and the food for our growing children. It's difficult. I'm just not used to not being able to provide for my family."

"The banks won't loan when you don't have an address. I would like to hear how are you doing, Bob? How is life for you now that you are a civilian, out of the Army and back on American soil?"

Bob quickly answered, "Sorry, but I need to move. I don't want to sit with my back to the door. I'm sure you have heard that I have PTSD."

Just then two pans were dropped in the kitchen. Bob jumped up and looked around to see if he can help anyone and then runs out of the door behind him and disappears into the night.

John assured me that he knew where Bob sleeps and would check on him and show where temporary help can be found. So my very special dinner ended with the gift of three new friends and living proof that there is not an easy answer for fixing the many problems we find on the street.

And The Winner Is . . .

By Betty Wyatt

Mrs. Baxter came through the front door in a rush, and tossed her purse and the stripped folder on the table in the foyer. She slipped out of her rain coat and hung it over the hall tree and walked swiftly to the kitchen. She was late and saw that home for mom at the school where she taught meant that dinner was going to be late.

Jim hated that. He had been asking her to quit teaching for the last five years. He wanted to come home to a house like his Mother ran—where Mom was a cook and a housekeeper and order and serenity rules. That wasn't true for Millie Baxter's house. The kids and her job came first. She glanced into the dining room and saw that Jason and Rosie were home and already settled into their homework.

"Hi, Mom, you're late," said Jason.

"Daddy called. He's going to be late, too. He has to finish a report and get it into the mail for Mr. Ryler," said Rosie.

"Thank you, Rosie, for the message, and thank you Guardian Angel for giving me a half-hour break for dinner, or maybe more. Now, what to fix?"

She stood in the center of the kitchen and opened the refrigerator door. The veggies from last night can go into a mixed green salad, if there is Ranch Dressing. Oh, good, there it is. Now, for the entre. Open the freezer and check the shelves. Saved by a Stouffers casserole of beef and noodles.

"How's the homework going tonight," she called.

"Okays," from both of them. "I can check it over in about 20 minutes if you're ready by then, and you can turn on the TV for your show on time. Don't rush though. Do a neat job of it."

There was a giggle from the dining room and Rosie whispered to Jason, "She says that every night!"

The casserole was transferred to one of their dishes and already was in the oven. The salad bowl was full of the chopped greens and she was arranging the left over veggies around the edges so it looked nice. The kids could have the ice cream drumsticks for desert.

The kids loved them and so did Jim, but he would never admit it. She took the loaf of sourdough out of the freezer and sliced it with the electric knife so it could be popped into the microwave to thaw and warm when Jim arrived home. The post office closed at 6:00 so it wouldn't be too much longer before she heard the car coming into the garage.

She headed into the dining room to do some homework check, but the kids had already folded and stacked their work. She said, "I guess I wasn't that late."

"No, we just thought we'd help you catch up," Jason said. "Rosie is going to help you fix the table, aren't you, Rosie?"

"It must be Star Wars night, but I'll be glad to help."

She went to the side board to get the table cloth. The two ladies of the house spread it, got out the dishes, set the table, and moved the flowers from the phone table to the center of the dining room table, and they were now ready for Daddy Jim.

Millie headed to the powder room to rinse her face, freshen her makeup, and comb her hair. Now she was ready for Daddy Jim, too.

227

She remembered her purse and folder on the hall table, and went to scoop them out of the hall and put them in the study for an evening session of correcting papers, but she noticed the spelling Bee Report was half way out of its folder. The list of final words was in plain sight and Jasons' homework was on the table ready for school in the morning. Had he seen it? He was on the team competing again this year. Should she ask him? Would he tell the truth? He really loved the competition and he was the winner of his grade in the regional war last year. What to do?

Jim came in the door from the garage at this moment. We hadn't heard the car so we hurried to the kitchen to greet him, but we did not bring up the spelling bee list. That was between her and Jason.

After a quick kiss, Jim's first words were, "Smells good. What's for dinner? I think it will be edible. Go have your glass of wine, and I will join you in a few moments."

"Jasons' show is just about over and Rosie helped me tonight, so we don't have to wait for Casper till the end."

"Does she still watch that silly thing?"

"There's nothing wrong living with an old favorite, Jim. You still watch "MASH" and that was years ago."

They had their wine, chatted about Jim's day and how school went for her, and as the Star Trek music swelled on the TV, she said, "Dinner Time."

Jim repeated her call. "Okay, Kids, Mom says its dinner time."

So they all met at the table and complimented Millie on the casserole and salad and the kids cheered for the drumsticks. Then it was Jason's turn to load and run the dishwasher with the rest scattered to do while whatever was on the docket—Rosie to the phone, Jim to his paper, Millie to grading papers, while Jason had not said a word.

In the morning it was the usual hassle. The kids went by bus first. Then Jim left and finally Millie put the rest of the breakfast clutter away, checked to see that Jason had fed the dog and let him out. Rosie had fed her cats and left them asleep on her bed. She then gathering her papers, the folio, and purse, and walked out to her car, and then drove on to school. Jason had not mentioned a thing.

When Millie parked and walked into the school office, she noticed Jason was in the principal's office. He was flushed and the principal was looking very concerned. Millie's heart sank. What had happened when she walked to Mrs. Scott's door?

"You should be very proud of your son, Jason, Mrs. Baxter. Do you want to tell your Mother what you just told me, Jason?"

"Yes, Ma'am. I saw the list for the spelling Bee sticking out of the folder last night when I put my homework on the table. I saw the words hydroponic, statistical, Hoodlum, candle, something, and then aardvark. Well, it had to be aardvark, because nothing else in my dictionary starts with two A's and one R, so I came in to Mrs. Scott's office to tell her I would have to resign from the team this year." He gulped, and bit his lips trying to hold back the rears of regret or nervousness.

Millie opened her arms and Jason stepped into them as she folded him in a big hug. "Oh, Jason I'm so proud of you. You handled your problem as an adult, and Father Christopher will be so proud of you. You have shown such moral fiber. Does Rosie know?"

"No, it was my problem and I kept it to myself. After I said my prayers last night I knew what I had to do."

Cleo, the Lonely Ghost

By Betty Wyatt

Cleo had never been so lonely. Living in the abandoned Light House on the tiny island in the middle of the Bay used to be fun. People used to come out in their boats and bring picnic lunches and bring kids and pets. Just having people around was stimulating, but no more.

The Island was once filled with chatter and laughter and, even if they ignored her, it was entertaining. Ghosts can only make themselves visible to someone who believes in them. Did you know that?

After the Coast guard abandoned the light house and no longer maintained it or the docks, boats stopped coming out. Oh, an occasional fisherman might come by and tie up for an hour or two. But in general there was no one to talk to. So Cleo moved into the lighthouse and mostly stayed up where the big Fresnel lens was and where the view of the bay was and the view of the village where she used to live.

Live, that was a lovely word and she really missed being alive. She had no idea how long she had been on the island, but she remembered the day she came here vividly. She thought it was probably a long time ago. There was no mirror she could look into to see if she had aged any. Ghosts can't cast an image in a mirror, you know. That's one of the ways you can tell if someone is a ghost.

She had come out with a group of friends. She was looking forward to her birthday next week when she would be 18, an official adult. The Bay was very rough and they were having trouble lining up with either of the docks as they came up onto the island. The waves were higher than she had ever seen them before and they came crashing on the rocky shore—that was the reason for the lighthouse.

Suddenly the boat reared up and Cleo fell out. She could hear the others screaming and she tried to swim, but her ankle was tangled in a fishing net that was wrapped around one of the dock pillars. She was being pulled down below the surface. She reached out to try to pull out of the heavy down as it twisted about the dock supports. She tried to scream but you can't do that under water.

She reached out to try to pull out of the heavy net, but it just grasped her waist and held her tighter. She could see signs of the ends of the pier that two of the boys had dived in and were searching for her, but they were looking in the waters further out, not in by the dock. Her struggling had exhausted her air and she realized she must have drowned. But she felt so alive—it's just that she seemed to float now, not having to strain and fight the net and the sea.

After a while she was aware that the boat had left. But later on she had no idea how many boats had come out, but they were all looking in the wrong area. She was now under the docks which gave her some protection from the pull of the currents.

The fishnet still enwrapped her in its tentacles. Eventually her friends gave up searching and she was left alone with the fish and other sea life. They made no effort to come near her or nibble on her body, which she understood was the fate of the drowned.

They were too aware of the net but she could not understand their talk, and there were squeaks of sympathy for her state. They explained that many drowned folks didn't complete their drowning, and although their body might disintegrate, their spirit body lived on often for many years. She cried a little but that was also consoled.

A Coast Guard crew came out in early fall to clear the fishnets caught in the area to make it safer for boats in the rougher winter seas. One group working on her dock unfurled the net in which she was tangled and there was great excitement at recovering her body.

Not a nibble on her with a little swelling from bumping into things recognizable, as the beautiful seventeen-year-old who had been missing for eight months. Her body was taken up to shore and then placed on one of the Coast Guard boats and taken to the main land. Her spirit moved to land and watched her funeral but no one seemed to see or be aware that she was there.

When it was over, she didn't stick around to hear what folks were saying about her. She felt sorry for her family, but that was depressing her terribly and she might start crying at all the lovely things they were saying about what she might have done had she lived. So she caught a breeze headed out over the Bay and learned that as a spirit, a ghost, she could navigate and was soon back on the island.

She wisely had checked the house for some clothes that weren't so tattered, for that would have aroused suspicion and might have gotten some perfectly honest living person accused of stealing her clothes. She was intending to be a good ghost because she had heard at one time that ghosts could leave their earth-bound condition if they saved a living person who was believed to be in "hazard or harm." Now all she needed to do was to find someone in such a state and save him or her.

Years passed and no such opportunity arose. She saved a lot of fish from nets and cared for birds that crashed into the island trees or rocks. But none of that worked and the few people who came out to her island seemed perfectly capable of taking care of themselves.

Then one day she was napping in the Lighthouse tower and glancing through one of the lighthouse broken windows (she did wish the Coast Guard would take better care of the place) and saw a boat hauling up to the docks. A young couple jumped up on the rickety dock and the young man reached down and pulled up a blanket and then dragged a picnic basket out and he and she headed to the grove of trees on the point.

Cleo couldn't see them from her perch so she went back to her nap. A bit later she heard the door at the base open and the man was trying to convince the girl that the stairs were safe and the view was worth the climb. It took them a while and Cleo slipped into a corner.

She could see what she thought was a man in his 30s or older. The girl on the other hand was quite young, still in her teens. He began to fold the blanket so they could recline on it.

When she had settled and was enjoying the view, he dropped down beside her and wrapped her in his arms and forced her down to the floor. The girl was obviously surprised and shocked by his action and she tried to scream, but who was there to help? It was clear what his intentions were, for he was already tearing at her blouse.

Cleo turned on all her power and moaned. This awakened one of the great-horned owls who shared her perch. He flew down across the struggling couple and out the broken window. Cleo moaned again, and

238

the man looked toward her dim corner. He dropped the girl and started to rise.

"Good, he believed." She moaned and floated up from the floor toward him slowly so that he might see the full effect of her translucent form. "What the hell?" he screamed.

He quickly closed his fly and headed for the steep twisting stairwell. The girl, who was still crying, was now trying to drag her torn blouse around her body and reclaim any other apparel he had peeled from her.

Now there was another problem. Did she believe? Cleo floated over to the girl who was struggling to her feet to clear with a puff of power to raise her up? Not too much power that would lift her from the floor, just enough to be erect.

"Oh my, god," She said. Looking about the room and spotting nothing she added, "Is this place haunted?"

Cleo could lift the blanket and make it float, and the girl broke into laughter, "It is, it's haunted and I have been saved by a friendly ghost like Casper."

A few moments pause and then, "Thank you, good ghost. May I see you as Scrooch saw his savers?"

With no effort at all, Cleo became visible and could talk to Debbie. They heard the boat's motor start. "I could stop him," Cleo said.

"No, let him go. I told my dad I was coming out here with Mr. Booth, my science teacher, on a field trip, so he'll know where I am."

"That was not a wise move, Debbie. I don't mean telling your family where you were going, but coming out here on a student field trip. Don't you know better?"

"Yes, but he said the other boat was leaving from a different dock and we'd all meet out here. You saved me, Cleo. How can I ever thank you?"

"You already have. I can now transcend Ghost Hood and rise to the next spirit level, training in angels in waiting. Just tell your Dad the truth to counter whatever lies Mr. Booth told when he got to shore. Don't spoil my transcendence, Debbie. I'm so tired of being in limbo. Be a wise woman, Debbie," as she floated out the window of the lighthouse.

Mast Head El Cajon News

By Betty Wyatt

Dear Editor:
You have probably not received this notice yet. Johnny's parents got it yesterday afternoon and called me at once. When I reached the grieving parents, the notification had been followed by a text from Wayne Peters, John's fellow Marine, and an El Cajon graduate. Details in this letter are from Wayne's text.

A little over a year ago you ran a story of El Cajon's soccer star, Johnny Jones, who was being scouted by pro-teams in his Jr. Year. His best friend, Wayne Peters, had graduated and joined the Marines in the previous year.

Instead of finishing college, Johnny had decided to leave school and join the Marines. An honor student and member of the Student council, this news came as a shock to the team, his fellow students, and the community. When we had a discussion about this decision, Johnny said, "There's more to life than kicking a ball, Dr. Manners."

After boot camp at Camp Pendleton, he was assigned to the Officer's Training Corps. After this basic course, he was posted to tank corps training for field service for several weeks and then shipped to Afghanistan. By almost a miracle, he was assigned to the same battalion that Wayne was serving in as lead sergeant. Their friendship picked up where it had left off on campus.

Last week in a special operation, Lt. Jones's tank was lead tank into action at a small village held by El Qada. Sergeant Peters was their walker who travels slightly ahead of the vehicle, spotting hazards. A new man, Taylor, was training as driver and when Peters waved to veer right, he became confused and veered left toward a clearing, instead of the building on the right. The tank hit two separate buried bombs spaced several feel apart, which flipped the tank onto its right side. The crew of three and Lt. Jones were severely shaken and sustained multiple blast injuries.

Sgt. Peters was injured by the force of the explosion, but retained consciousness and ran to the hatch on the top of the tank which was now on its side, parallel to the ground. As he endeavored to open it from the outside, Lt. Jones was on the inside working to open the hatch. When the hatch was open, Jones dragged out the two crewmen who were unconscious and limp to the hatch opening, one at a time, boosted them from inside to Wayne who pulled them out from the tank, which was beginning to burn.

Inside the tank, Johnny was endeavoring to remove the unconscious driver from his seating restraints, who was bleeding badly from a head injury. He finally released him from the seat and with difficulty dragged him to the hatch and boosted him through the opening and then crawled on the tanks side to try to get through the hatch.

The tank interior was now in full flame and his uniform was on fire. Wayne returned to the hatch when he realized Johnny was in trouble. He hauled his screaming friend and dropped him to the ground where he rolled him on the dirt road endeavoring to put out the burning clothes.

By now the rest of the company had drawn close and medics were running to the three injured crewmen. The enemy troops were pouring from the village and the Marines had formed an attack line. The flipped tank was a hazard to both sides, and it finally exploded, blasting metal in all directions at both lines of the Al-Qada and Marines.

The medics had moved the injured to the shelter of the buildings just before the blast. The convoy had called for chopper support and during the skirmish a medic-chopper landed and took the injured Marines on board and to the hospital.

The three crewmen had a variety of injuries— broken ribs, facial lacerations, and the driver was the most serious, with brain injury and spinal injury. How Wayne did what he did was almost impossible, since he had a severe hip injury from the initial blast that capsized the tank and blew him up against a building. Lt. Jones had very serious burns over most of his body and several fractures. He died in the chopper on the way to the hospital.

The Battalion Commander, Col. Jed Smithson, has nominated Sgt. Wayne Peters and Lt. Johnny Jones for Silver Stars, and has requested forms to nominate Lt.

Johnny Jones for the Congressional Medal of Honor. All of the wounded will receive Purple Hearts, of course.

The injured have been transported to Germany for more care. Lt. Jones's body is being prepared for shipment home, where a decision is being made by his parents, Marsha and Christopher Jones, whether the burial will be at Arlington or here at home in the El Cajon Veterans Memorial Park.

A Memorial Service for Lt. Johnny Jones will be held at El Cajon College and he will be given a Bachelor of Science degree along with his fellow classmates in June. This is when he would have graduated with honors if he had not withdrawn early from his junior year. The class, all students, and staff of El Cajon College, send their deepest sympathies and great pride in their son to Martha and Christopher Jones.

Poppa

By Betty Wyatt

(A true story)

On the town roster of voters, he was Mr. William
S. Purgitt. To his wife he was Will. To folks who
thought they knew him, but really didn't, he was Bill.
My father called him dad, but to me as a youngster, he
was just Poppa, the perfect Grandfather.

He was already white haired when he came into
my life's consciousness. He must have been born in
the late 1860's because my Dad was born in 1888. My
Father was his first born son and a little bit of a
favorite in the family. I inherited some of that extra
love as my Father's first child.

Mother and I lived with Momma and Poppa when
Dad was in the Western Mediterranean Fleet on sea
duty, shortly after my birth. They had created a one
room apartment for Mother and me in the big

bedroom with a kitchenette and balcony that shared the one bathroom in the house.

I have some vague memories of the time we lived there, most of them sitting on Poppa's lap in the part-time dining room with the accordion table sitting in the bay window. When it was not involved in hosting 10 or 12 people with the table extended, we would call it a family room. We didn't have a fireplace, just a big brown coal stove with an Eisenglass window that you could watch the flames flickering over the coals.

I think Mother and Grandmother were in the adjacent kitchen, cooking whatever meal we had that could be served at the long oak table which would feed the hands at harvest and planting time. Most family meals were taken there.

It must have been Poppa's job to sit in his chair by the stove with me on his lap to entertain me with songs and stories. If it was after supper, I probably fell asleep to his soft voice and the flickering flames.

When Dad got back from Turkey and points north, we moved to the Great Lakes, and from then on we only saw my Grand Parents on visits in the summer. No more dancing flames in the big brown stove, but lots of time with Poppa. He loved kids and we were always trailing after him when he was home. So I had to share him with resident and visiting cousins.

He was a good man. Like everyone else in Bayard, he worked at the mine on the Maryland side of the Potomac. Bayard is in West Virginia, although it started out in Virginia. It's an old mine dangerous to work in, with no electric carts or lights inside, except at the elevators that took the miners up and down to the various shafts and also hauled the horses that pulled the carts up and down each day.

No little electric trains, no powerful electric drills. It was still a blast pick and shovels mine—or so Poppa told me. Some nights they didn't even bring the horses up to the surface. There were stalls near the larger opening to the surface elevator which had been powered by a very noisy generator you could hear over in town.

Poppa didn't work below, for he was a supervisor or something bigger up top, but he had worked the shafts when he was young and he felt for the horses in their terrible environment. Every weekend he would bring two of them home to graze in the pasture by the house. They had to wade across the river at a shallow point and he would wash them down in the stream.

249

He kept a bucket and brushes at the ford to do the job. I can remember watching him do it once (daddy took me down to the banks to see it). The horses emerged sooty grey from the mine and emerged from their baths as a white and grey horse. They weren't ponies like the Welsh still use—they were big horses.

Then it was up the hill, cross the road, open the gate into the four acres of pasture, climb the bank into the pasture, and roll in the grass for the horses. You could see that they had found heaven. Poppa would close the gate and then fill the feed box that was up hill from the road. The horses would be there for the weekend and if I was lucky, I got a bare back ride on the big white one, with Poppa walking by the horse to hold me, or catch me if I started to fall off. Then the cousins would arrive, maybe with a dad and the other horse to provide rides.

When I was older, 10 or 11, and we came to visit, Poppa no longer worked at the mine. He had opened the only gas station in town. It was a converted barn on the river side of the road that was used for milk cows when they were still operated by the farm. The hill was very steep as it stepped down to the river, so the back end of the barn was on a heavy wall for support. It made a fine garage, and by being on a slope, you could drive a car into it after you had lifted the covering over the pit to service a car from below.

He sold Gulf gasoline to cars and it didn't make the family wealthy by any means, but it kept several men in the town employed during the depression. Poppa would carry the sales records across the road at night and put them into a machine that printed out a receipt for the customer and a record for Momma, the book keeper in the family.

In the early years of the deep depression, he would still walk down to the river and meet a worker who had led two horses from the mine. He would take them from him and wash them down as he had done for years and lead them up to the pasture. When the mine closed, he bought one of the old horses so it could spend its last days at ease on his farm.

That was when the town really suffered. Many folks just walked away from their homes and headed east where there were jobs. On the other hand, Eleanor saw that Franklin got the Alleghany mountain towns and others across the country electrified. Grandmother was afraid of it and hated putting wires in the walls of the house. She wanted them on the outside, but Poppa ruled on that one and the gas lights were turned off in the house, but gas was kept on for part of the coal stove which had always used gas for summer cooking and also for the two water heaters. The lamplighter lost his job and the streets glowed at night with Mr. Edison's invention. The remaining homes also blossomed with porch lights which they had never had in the gas days.

I never saw my grandparents after I graduated from High School. That summer was the last whole family trek east in the big bash, so my memories are frozen in the time. It's as though I have lived in three centuries, because Bayard was still living in the 80s whenever I visited it as a little kid, though I was living in the 20th century and now in the 21st century. Can that be?

Reflecting On Life on a Hot Day

By Betty Wyatt

It had been several days ago. The Girls got together to just talk. They all lived in the same Senior Housing, but they were scattered among the several buildings and never really got to find out what made the individual members of the Art Class click, or maybe she meant tick. Somehow you may have taken a wrong turn some place in your bright future and now you've not only lost it, but nothing has turned out as you had hoped for 20 or 30 years ago?"

I'm Sara, and you will notice that I don't say anything in this chat session. Instead, I'm recording the ladies' comments on my phone. Now a week or so later, I'm listening to the event and pondering the talk.

It's a very warm day and I'm sitting on my balcony enjoying a light breeze that makes it livable, while watching the birds flying from feeder to trees and up and down the dry creek bed.

Vivian, our eldest, was the first to speak up. "I may have made a turn or two in my 90 years but I can't imagine being in a better spot than I am now. Nice apartment, efficient cleaning service, classes I enjoy, great people for company, and good food. Compared to some periods in my past, this is paradise!"

Gladys chimed in. "Well, maybe not paradise, but sure better than a generation or so ago. Look at the life your grandmother had to live for her final days. She was forced to live with her son's family in a run-down house with no TV, no public transport, and not even a radio to bring the world into her life.

"Half the people we knew were on relief or trying to get on relief. Our son was unemployed and his wife was working in a dime store so they could have some cash. Grandma was stuck with the household chores and was taking care of the five kids.

"No, I'll take this life over that one any day, and it could have been my lot. I was going to drop out of high school so I could lend a hand but the Principal talked me out of it and saw that I got a scholarship to a business school. I've never forgotten her kindness and wisdom."

"Boy, I never think of you that way, Gladys," Sheila said, shaking her head. "Your speech is so refined, and you are so beautifully groomed."

"Well, I was lucky enough to be motivated and I landed a job in an attorney's office where everyone else had gone to college, and they encouraged me to do the same. So it was, one class at a time, and I eventually got my degree and moved up the promotion ladder and married the nicest man in the world and was able to help Grandma get out of her situation."

"How about you, Clara? You've got a contented look on your face. Is everything OK for you in your life?" said Debby, who started this round of questioning.

"Who me? Yea I had a very full life. Three husbands—one killed in WW2, a second one by a truck driver crippling him for the remainder of his short life by a crash, and number three by an attorney who got me a five million dollar settlement based on number two's crash.

"I've worked as a nurse's aide most of my life and raised two boys who are doing OK. One is a pro athlete and the other is a coach. They come home sometimes for barbecues. They are good kids and each have married and each have had a child. I wouldn't say things worked out as planned in my life but I'm happy to be here most of the time. I try not to think too much about my past when I had a lot of dark days, but it seems to have turned ok for me."

"OK, Debby. You started this round of yesterday chat. What makes you think your life has turned out wrong. What had you planned?"

"Oh, I planned to be somebody, and instead I'm nothing. I never married because no one asked me. I guess that's what I regret most of all. I planned to write a great book and all I have to show for my writing is a drawer full of rejection slips.

"I had a nice little house for most of my life that my parents gave me, but I was never able to fill it with friends. I seem to lack all social skills and it's that way here too. No one comes to my room and a couple of people have asked me to join them for dinner, but only once—and tears began to course down her cheeks."

Vivian passed a box of tissues toward her. "I have a question for you, Debby? How many people have you asked to join you for dinner? I mean new people who haven't formed bonds yet?"

"None, I guess."

Vera, who had some poems published, said, "I'd love to see some of your writing. I gave up trying to write the great American Novel. Now I just try to tell a good story and that's worked well for me. Maybe you've got some good stories in that stuff and now that you are older you can bring more depth to them than a teenager. And for heaven's sake, don't stop making plans. All of us here have plans—to go shopping, to have a good meal out, to see a play, or go to a Museum. Life's still out there waiting to be sampled."

Sitting here on my balcony, watching the birds flitting from tree to tree and reflecting on the lives of my fellow artists, I think the girls have done pretty well with their lives and they illustrate that basically you've got to try and not just let life roll along through your years.

The Best Laid Plans

By Betty Wyatt

Roy and Roxanne met while exchange students at the University of Mexico, the oldest Institution of higher learning in the Western hemisphere. They were just two among a hundred but it was really a fluke that they met. He was studying in part of the modern campus in a lab with a bunch of physicists. She was studying literature and history in one of the 15th Century clusters.

Roy Baxter and a couple of his fellow Nerds heard that the women were all staying in one of the upscale hotels and decided to check out their compatriots. Roxanne was being hassled while in the pool by another male who had discovered the same information when they arrived, and Roy stepped up with a pair of tall drinks on a tray which he placed on a table and then offered Roxanne two hands to pull her from the pool. As she emerged he saw the great legs of a swimmer and tan of an outdoor girl.

"You must be a California Girl," he sort of sang, as Roxanne thanked him.

"Then you must be a knight in a tee shirt who rescued me from the evil past," she answered, and so their friendship began.

They quickly learned she was down from Stanford and that he was from Berkeley. Only a Bay kept them apart and when they returned to their campuses from Mexico, they kept up the contact every other week of the fall term. So many interests they had in common: hiking, theatre, and concerts, plus soccer and football games. So, by Christmas they were engaged. They both graduated in June and were married a few days after that.

Roxanne found a job at a start up in Fremont, IPSY Daisy (International Personnel System) as a copy writer. Roy decided to stay and get his Masters, which he had started working on the last year as an undergraduate, with his advisor's consent.

They found an affordable apartment north of Fremont and it was an easy commute for both of them. Roy had a carpool to the Lab, and Roxanne or as she was now known by her fellow Daisy employees, Roxy, just hopped on BART and got off one block from work.

Then a very nice thing happened. The management of IPSY Daisy said that any of the new hires who passed up their first year's vacation, would get 4 weeks in their second year. Roy and Roxy were ecstatic. They started planning at once in the first year. Since they both spoke passable Spanish, it would be Latin America, of course. It had everything they were passionate about—mountain trails, rich bird life (Roy), ruins (Roxy), spectacular cities with theatre, concerts, and soccer.

The maps and brochures took over what was meant to be a dining room table for when they entertained. They had all their meals in the kitchen on a card table.

They decided against a travel agent. They just wanted to go where their spirit took them. Since they had already spent 6 months in Mexico, they decided to skip that and start with a flight to Guatemala, rent a car, and then drive south to Argentina. The Pan-American Highway was supposed to be finished by then as well.

When they told Roy's parents, the Baxter's, about their plans, they thought it was a wonderful idea.

"When I was traveling all the time, shooting my documentaries, we found American Express very helpful, not just for traveler's checks, but for trip arrangements, like car rental and reservations."

So the young couple decided to check out American Express's multi services, only to meet their first shocks. A massive counterfeit operation in traveler's checks had hit the company in Latin America. Most companies down there would no longer accept their checks. Instead they were offering a pay up front plan of determining what your expenses would run, deposit the money with them, and they would issue a special credit card that paid your depts.

It was sort of like having a trust account. Roy looked at Roxanne and they both shook their heads. They had not counted on paying flights, car rentals, and accommodations in advance. They were banking funds, but they would never have enough by their departure date to pay everything up front. Roxanne's unused salary during the month was supposed to cover most post bills, but this was a major blow.

Oh, and in none of the Latin American countries could you take a rental car out of the country. Too many emigrants drove them as close to the US border as they could get to, and then abandoned the car. Then you turned in your car where you rented it, and paid for it before you left the country. What a blow to drifting it where your spirit takes you.

Headlines on the paper that night screamed about a disastrous volcano. Eruption in Guatemala near the Pan-American Highway had killed hundreds of evacuees. Three blows in one day. They would now have to skip Guatemala. Why not fly to Argentina and work their way North instead.

They started studying the maps again. Take Argentina south to Tierra del Fuego along the coast and then back along the mountain front. Then flip a coin for Iguacu Falls in Brazil, and take Argentina over the Andes to Chile. It sounded great.

Meantime, Roxy had been striking out on tropical clothing in the local stores, so she had ordered a selection from catalogs. Her mother had warned her that if she wanted to go this route to do so early because of slow deliveries, back orders, and the need to exchange anything that wasn't right by mail.

Mrs. Bouvier was so right. She found some beautiful clothes in tropical weight but when the shipments arrived, the clothes were not as represented in the catalogs. The colors were off and many things on page one described as same hues as the clothes on page 20 were from different rainbows. The garment weights were the same as Kohl's or Macys—not cool weaves at all. So back they went one shipment at a time with replacements in different sizes or colors ordered or just plain cancelled.

She did find a fantastic pair of knee high boots that were water proof, light weight, a blend of Kevlar and nylon that would be impenetrable by snakes and leaches, or other hazards of the bush, ticks or swamps. They were woven of green and black fabric with the shoe part in a special rubber that looked like leather. She got a whole lot of compliments on them when she wore them to work one day, when the streets were flooded, AND THEY WERE COMFORTABLE— something rare in knee highs.

They had rechecked their maps. Roy spent one night figuring the mileage they were planning to drive and was shocked. He hadn't realized how big the area was and then he checked with Google on petrol prices by the liter, rather than by the gallon, and then really went into shock.

They had also had their first found of shots that week, and Roy was really sick from the Yellow Fever injection. His Mother said, "I'm sorry, dear. I was terribly ill with Yellow Fever on our first trip to Panama. Do you think that could have made you sensitive? Check with your doctor, honey. What other shots are you getting?"

Roxy had hers the next day and was allergic to something in them, because she blossomed with hives that were driving her crazy as she sat at the card table sending one more pants suit back to its catalog home. It had been back ordered and was late arriving. Flipping the container to tape the back, she knocked her cup of coffee on the table toward some papers she had brought home to work on. Sopping up the mess and rescuing her papers, she moaned, "Oh, this stupid trip. I wish it would just go away."

"What did you just say?" Roy asked from the living room.

Her voice a little tremulous, she answered, "I hoped you hadn't hear that. This wonderful adventure has taken over our lives. Nothing is the same."

"Isn't that what a vacation is for? To make changes in your life, open up new horizons, and stir things up?"

"We haven't been to a show, or a concert, or a game since we started planning this thing ten months ago. Now you're sick and I'm a mess with hives. We haven't even had drinks with our friends or seen anyone for dinner. I wish it were over," she said, and started to cry.

Roy hobbled to her side and wrapped his arms about her. "We're just trying to do too much, love. Let's cut it down to one country! Or we could go to Europe or England. Their infrastructure is better, rentals aren't as difficult, and if we cancelled all of this," and he waved at the maps, brochures, and spilled coffee. "We have trip insurance and could get all of our money back, pay for the new trip, and skip the rest of the shots."

And he raised her chin and kissed her.

"Oh, Roy could we?"

"Yep, in the morning."

So they rose early. They phoned in sick to where they had to be and jumped on BART to head to Oakland to cancel a year and half of planning and getting their money back. It was a frantic morning, but they did it. They then had lunch at Jack London Square (it seemed appropriate) while they discussed what they wanted to do in Britain.

They took a cab to start the Visa work for Britain and the EU. It had made travel from country to country in Europe easier. They would spend two weeks in Britain and they would pick a country to spend ten days and then fly home with a couple of days to recover. The whole thing was done at one travel agency in a half day since they had the passports and all that was out of the way. The agency would confirm their reservations on Monday and they had their tickets to fly now. There was a "Remember Rock" concert in Oakland tonight and tickets were available to hear some of the old great names, so they went.

A few weeks later they were hopping in a cab in front of their apartment with their luggage and headed to SFO airport over the Dumbarton Bridge. As they reached the west side of the Bay they were merging into the freeway when a bus came barreling out of nowhere. Weaving and rocking and going at least 70 miles per hour, cars were scattered behind them, but they were not aware of it. Their driver was trying to pull to the right off the freeway but the railing had pinned them. The bus which was apparently empty had hit them broadside and knocked the cab loose. The cab rolled down the slope of the freeway.

The bus's engine was still running, though it was pinned by the steel Stanton which had bent over it, continued to sway and rock. One of the police cars that had been pursuing the runaway, pulled onto the back of the bus and the two officers scrambled down to the partially crushed cab. They got one door open on the left side and pulled Roy and Roxy out and then smashed the drive window to drag the driver out after slitting the seat belt. They dragged the unconscious passengers some distance from the cab, just as the bus finally broke loose allowing it to roll down the grade and crash on top of the cab.

A chase helicopter that had been following the events had radioed for help and the ambulance was unbelievably fast in getting there.

A week later, Roy and Roxy were sharing a room at Seton Hospital, the closest medical facility next to the Airport. Roxy who had been on the right side of the cab had a broken right shoulder and arm plus multiple cuts, bruises, and abrasions. Roy, who had been in the left seat, had a broken left hip, left leg, ribs, and possible concussion. His injuries were primarily from when the bus crashed into them, hooked and dragged the cab. Roxanne's were from the roll down the hill. They had both been cut free from the cab by one of the officers. Roxy was the last to be removed, because in essence she was on the bottom.

A nurse popped into the room to raise the heads of the beds.

"You have company," she announced. "Officers O'Rourke and Chang are here to check on you. They pulled you from the cab and a man from the DA's office is with them to get our statements. Are you up to giving your statement," she said as she scooted from the room.

The two patients tried to get a little higher in their beds to greet the man they most wanted to see. Officer O'Rourke had saved them from sure death if they had still been in the cab when the bus rolled onto the slope and flattened the cab before it burst into flames. It was a spectacular scene on the 10:00 News.

Officer O'Rourke came to Roy's bed side and took his extended hand. "There is no way to ever thank you adequately for your sacrifice and risk. May God reward you," Roy said through his bandages, clutching the Officer's hand.

Roxanne reached out to the officer who was visibly very moved by viewing the two of them. He came to her bed side and she pulled him closer to kiss him on his cheek. "What can I ever say to you, and she broke down in tears."

"It was all in the line of duty, but I'm sure glad you are both still with us. I'm sorry about your luggage, but nothing was salvageable, I'm afraid. I gather you were leaving for a vacation."

"Yes," Roy spoke up. "Four weeks in Europe."

O'Rourke had returned to Chang's side. Chang handed him one of the photos she had been holding. Both officers were shaking their heads. He handed the photo to Roy, who broke into laughter when he saw it. He then passed it toward Roxanne and Chang, who had come up to the bad handed it to Roxanne. The photo showed the bus with a giant ten foot poster on its side saying "SEE AMERICA FIRST" with photos of the National Parks splayed across it.

Roxanne managed a smile and said, "I think we get the message."

Family Quarry

A Four Chapter Story created by Four Different Authors (Each builds their story upon the previous person's work)

The Family Quarry

A Story of the Lazy S

By Chuck Northup

Nestled against the western slope of the Rockies in Western Colorado lies the ancestral home of the Jenkins. The plot is over 250 acres, which lies in the high plain altitude and heads up into the foothills. The home is a Queen Anne style mansion built before 1900 that contains fifteen rooms on two floors. It has the typical circular corner tower of that architectural era with porches surrounding most of the home on both floors—the upper ones becoming balconies for the bedrooms.

Downstairs held the "working" parts of the home—a kitchen with a pantry, a maid's quarters, a living room, a dining room, a parlor, a study, an entry, a main bathroom, a mudroom, and other nooks and crannies. There was plenty of room for a large family, and at the time of building, the number of children exceeded a dozen (normal for the time). Upstairs contained the bedrooms and more bathrooms.

Great Grandfather Jenkins built this beautiful home in 1876 to show off his earned wealth, and to have a good place to raise his family. The ranch was large enough to have cattle that could graze up into the hills, and still had enough flat land for good pasture and buildings. It was all fenced in to prevent wandering animals, both wild and tame. However, an occasional deer would enter, only to become part of the menu later. Grandfather Jenkins also raised a plot of alfalfa that produced good profits, as well as provided plenty of feed for his cattle.

Grandfather Jenkins' cattle were branded with the letter S lying on its side, which were called the Lazy S symbols. Therefore, his ranch was known by that name. Around the bars in the nearby town of Dorado, the name became "Lazy Ass!" and that name was often used, because cattle ranchers did little for most of the year, until roundup time.

The property was always left to the eldest son, much to the chagrin of the other offspring, and eventually two generations later the property fell into the hands of Paul Jenkins, who was very astute about running a business. In his capable hands the ranch prospered. He added horse stalls to the large barn and began a riding stable. He took in students and taught riding, while his wife Cherly taught dressage and did some bookkeeping.

Paul and Cherly met in Colorado State University. He was pursuing a degree in Business Administration and she was pursuing a degree in Accounting. They found they both loved horses and she dreamed of working with them with dressage that she had enjoyed as a young lady before college. He in turn was inheriting the Lazy S ranch and wanted to expand it for better profitability. They finished college together and she went to work with a CPA firm and he returned to the ranch to work with his elderly father.

Before long, Paul approached his father about starting a riding stable that would involve some outlay in capital, such as buying horses, expanding the barn, and building an arena with a waiting lounge for parents or others. Pleased by the attention Paul took toward the ranch, his father easily agreed.

The two proceeded to build the arena combined with a lounge and office. The lounge had a large window looking out onto the arena so parents could watch their youngsters learn to ride as they waited.

There were restrooms for men and women and a setup for coffee or tea. They removed the office from the home, so that business could be conducted without going into the main house.

When Paul started the business, he began small with only a few horses, but eventually he grew to the capacity of ten that the converted barn could hold. He also improved the trails into the hills on his property, so more experienced riders could take longer rides out of danger.

Cherly worked for several years at a CPA firm while seeing Paul most of the time. Soon the two were engaged and were then married within eight months. In the interim, Cherly moved in with him at his family home. By this time Paul's three brothers and sisters had moved out, creating plenty of room for them all to live.

While Paul's mother and father were driving home from church one Sunday morning, they were struck and killed by another driver. This sad event left Paul completely in charge of the Lazy S ranch, and now he was on his own to make a success of the farm. Cherly agreed to take over the small bookkeeping chores and she divided her time between the riding office and her home. It was not long before babies started arriving, but that did not stop her bookkeeping, because it only required mostly sitting down.

The couple decided to stop at three children — Erin, a boy; Lois, a girl; and Irene, another girl. During their growing up days, the riding school succeeded nicely. It produced a profit from the beginning, mostly because the former ranch business covered all of the costs of the new building. Paul still maintained the cattle, but kept a lesser number in order to cut down on the roundup work involved.

As the kids grew older, Cherly took more interest in building up a dressage section at their school. At first, she could spend only a little time with it, since she was needed with their children, but when all of them entered school, she had more time. To increase the hours available to teach, they added a roof to the arena, with lights for night lessons. With this addition, they were able to add several employed people to their business.

The advantageous part of teaching dressage is that the students owned their own horses. The barn was enlarged again to accommodate the extra horses, and now the ranch could charge rent for boarding horses, thus bringing in more income. The students also needed trailers to haul their horses to and from various shows, so the Jenkins provided a paved area for the trailers, and charged rent for that space as well.

As the Lazy S ranch grew over the years, it became known as an equestrian center and gained recognition throughout southwestern Colorado. After a while, with over forty horses on the ranch, they had to hire more trainers. Meanwhile, their three children had grown, attended college, and moved on to different locations.

Erin was in line to inherit the ranch, but his thoughts were elsewhere. He had decided to go into Engineering and ended up buying a small solar panel manufacturing company in Vermont. Lois married, had two children of her own, and lived in Australia. Irene had a beautiful voice and always wanted to go into opera. When she was still a mere teenager, she moved to Italy to study voice, and she met a man who was an opera notable, whom she later married. She continues to live in Italy today.

One evening at the dinner table Cherly said to Paul, "I saw Ethyl, our neighbor, in town today and I invited she and her husband to have dinner with us on Saturday night. Is that okay with you?"

"Yes, I haven't seen them in a long time. I wonder how Harry is doing. The last time I saw him he was having some knee problems. I hope he can walk better now."

"I'm not sure, but since Ethyl agreed, I think he's well enough to come over. She didn't say anything about his knees. I want to dig out those old photos we have and go through them. Ethyl and Harry are in lots of them. We can look at them and have some laughs together."

On Saturday evening, Ethyl and Harry Bothwell got into their old car to drive the short distance to their neighbor's home. They pulled up in front of the Jenkin's home after traveling through the archway, a large Lazy S brand over the roadway at the entrance. The house had an additional picket fence surrounding the immediate yard and then three or four steps leading up to the porch that encircled the major part of the perimeter. The porch also had a white railing intercepted by several pillars supporting the porch roof and upper balcony. The roof was studded with numerous gables to allow windows for the upstairs rooms. To the left was a cylindrical tower with windows on all faces.

The Bothwells tapped on the stained-glass front door and were immediately greeted by the Jenkin's, who ushered them in and took off their coats and jackets. They all greeted one another with hugs and handshakes and Emily said, "Dinner won't be ready for a few minutes, so please come into the study for a drink."

The study had one wall covered with books and several comfortable chairs into which they all seated themselves. A maid brought in glasses, and Paul asked what everyone would like to drink. He mixed drinks for all of them as they exchanged small talk.

Harry asked, "Who is taking care of the horses?"

"We have a stable boy who does that work," Paul answered, "But the horses are all okay for the night, since they don't need any care while they sleep. The boy makes sure they have plenty of food and good bedding."

"That must save you a lot of work."

"My work comes during the day," Cherly said, "and sometimes in the evening. I get young students during the day, but folks who work elsewhere often come by at night for lessons. All that does keep me busy, but tonight I have the night off."

Cherly added, "My students are all daytime people, but I'm beginning to get requests for evening classes as well, although I'm not sure I want to work both days and nights."

At that point, the maid appeared and announced that dinner was ready. The four friends casually walked into the dining room and sat down to a fine meal with wine. Conversation was about the goings-on in both families.

"Have you heard from your daughter in Italy, lately," Harry asked.

Cherly replied very proudly. "She's hooked up with a nobleman in Naples. He sent photos, and he's quite handsome. I don't know how far that will go, but she's reveling in the experience right now. She wrote of going to fancy homes and elegant restaurants with him. It sounds exciting."

"Wow, you may end up with some royalty in your family! What about your other daughter who is in Australia?"

"She and her husband are getting along well. They now have two children, and she's pretty well used up taking care of them and their house. If we get a few weeks of vacation from our own business, we plan to take a trip down there to visit them. I'm anxious to see them all again.

"And speaking of all," she continued, "we want to see Erin and his wife also. We may take a trip to Vermont on a long weekend. That's not nearly so far, and we can fit it in easily between classes here."

"It's really nice that you can visit most of your kids," said Harry. "We're lucky that ours live nearby so we can see them all the time as well."

"When I saw you at the market the other day," Cherly said, "I remembered those old photos we took years ago, so I scrounged around until I found them and thought we should share them with you. Look at this album. You'll get some good laughs."

Cherly produced a photo album and started flipping pages. Immediately the others got up and gathered around her, looking over her shoulders while speaking about the pictures.

"There are all the kids playing together at Lakeview Park," she laughed. "Do you remember, Paul, how one of the girls got stuck up in a tree, and you had to climb up to get her."

"Yes, and I nearly fell out of the tree myself," Paul exclaimed.

They proceeded through many photos, and finally came to three figures in a blizzard. "This is an exciting one," Cherly gushed. "It was during the blizzard of 2003, when the winds blew at a high rate sweeping down from Wolf Creek Pass, piling up almost three feet of snow everywhere. The animals needed food, so Paul, Rein, and the stable boy went out into that storm. I could barely see them, but I snapped this picture from the kitchen to be able to remember how bad it had gotten. They had to go out to the barn, that was only about a hundred feet from the house, but they couldn't even see it through the storm. The weather bureau claimed it was the worst blizzard since 1913 when they had four feet of snow build up."

"That sure was some blizzard," Harry recalled. "I remember we lost some animals in that storm. It was very serious."

The Family Quarry

The Grandsons make a Proposal
By Kent Humpal

Paul often thought about his dad, Uncle Grant, and Sherman Jenkins. They had been the true factors in enlarging and improving the old ranch and homestead. Reminiscing as he worked about the grounds, he recalled the family stories about the original homestead and his grandparent's struggles in starting up the Lazy S ranch.

After the Civil War, his Great Grandpa Josh had come to Colorado to seek his fortune. He was young and had only served in the final campaigns of the war. He hadn't wanted to go back to Iowa to the farm, so after mustering out of the 1st Wisconsin Cavalry, he went home to see his family and headed west, ending up in Southwest Colorado.

Living nearby, but not settling into Dorado, the largest settlement, he found no fortune, but rather lots of hard work. An opportunity was presented to him about a partnership in a two-man freighting business into the back country. This would keep him busy and allow him to look around the country for other enterprises.

Great Grandpa Josh had somehow been trading and supplying goods to the mountain Indians in their isolated villages. They had early on realized that accommodating the white trappers and allying themselves with the Mormon leaders of Utah gave them a unique status and protection from other tribes and white encroachment. Josh soon found himself totally accepted and beneficial.

The trading visits to the Ute villages brought him into contact with an ex-trapper/hunter living in the village. Here was where he met Great Grandma Brighty. The trapper had married into the tribe as a thing of convenience, only to have it become a loving, caring relationship. They had tried living in the white communities for a while, but found his wife's people more accepting. Their two sons had been educated by Mormon missionaries.

They had moved on to work on ranches and guide migrants and hunters. The youngest child, a girl who was an old maid by tribal standards, lived with her parents in the cabin her father had built. The Ute-Shoshana plus Scotts-Irish mix had given her an exotic look—she was a tall, slender woman with an erect carriage—a head above most of the Ute women. More hazel than brown eyes, set off by natural arched brows and a mane of unbound hair of dark brown with a hint of Irish-Auburn when struck by the sun.

If not beautiful, she was prettier than anyone Josh Jenkins had seen in the local towns and sparse ranches. Like her brothers, she had been educated by the Mormon wives and missionaries. She had opened a school in the village hoping to keep out the male owners and white supremacists from the government school.

Josh began bringing in books and school supplies and hanging around Bright Bird McDowd. Like her brother, she had both Indian and Anglo names. Bright Bird sings to the morning sun. Also called Mary McDowd, she preferred Bright Bird, or as John called her, Brighty. They were married the following spring.

Leaving Brighty with her family, Josh went off to file a homestead claim on the land that became the headquarters of the present Lazy S ranch. With range rights and government leases, Josh added several thousand acres and water rights to the 640 acres of the main ranch.

287

In a few years, realizing that he needed to legalize his claims and water rights as well as upgrade his cattle, Josh started looking for financial help. A downturn in the economy and a severe winter had made the banks reluctant to lend money to the ranchers. However, complaining to his father in law brought unexpected results.

The older man, having been in the hills and mountains hunting and trapping with the Ute and Shoshoni, he thought there might be a solution. Discussing the idea with the tribal elders, Hunts with Eyes (Archie McDowd) gave them an idea to lead Josh to the site of a gold-bearing outcrop kept secret and hidden from inquisitive white eyes.

Blind folded and having sworn a binding oath, Archie and a small group of elders led Josh to the site. After several days on horseback the party arrived. Clearing the site of rubble, medium boulders, some small trees, and shrubs that had sprung up, and again having Josh repeat the oath to never reveal the source and take only what he needed and not try to find the spot again, they showed him the outcropping of rotten quartz.

When under cover, Josh could see that the quartz extended back into the hillside. True to his word he began, with help, to pick up small nuggets and flakes that had eroded and dropped off. The weathered and porous vein yielded enough to fill several leather pouches. Using the point of his Barlow knife, he pried open a few more pieces with the white quartz clinging to it. Remembering his oath and not wanting to dishonor his father in law or himself, Josh quit midway through the next day—signaling that he was ready to leave.

The return trip took several days longer. Utes, surrounded by the high mountains, with peaks 10,000 to 14,000 feet high, showed the hunters that on the way home there was an opportunity to hunt the elusive Mountain Sheep they revered. Coming back to the camp with some heads and hides of the sheep and elk meat, they were greeted heartily by their families. Thus came about the real beginning of the Lazy S ranch.

Later, riding the range, checking water holes, and rounding up some cattle, Josh began recognizing some Tourain and an occasional landmark. Being an honorable man, however, he kept his oath, but when confiding with Brighty about it, they decided to record what he could remember, sketch some of the landmarks, and leave a description of the trip for the record. Keeping his oath, however, he never looked for the spot again.

One morning in the late Fall, after the students had left and most of the privately owned horses had been transported to warmer climes avoiding harsh weather, Paul heard a truck coming off the county road onto the rock and gravel drive. Sauntering out of the tack room he went to greet his visitors.

"Hello, gentlemen, what can I do for you?"

Two men in their mid to late 20s emerged from the truck. They had to be brothers. Same builds, same eyes, and same brown hair with reddish tint, they certainly looked familiar.

"Uncle Paul, I know it's been a while. It's your nephews, Gus and Fred."

"Great Zeus, you were both in high school when I last saw you two. How's your Dad and Mom?"

Looking them over, Paul said, "Which of you is August or Fred? You look so much alike I can't tell."

"Well, the homely runt next to me is Fred, and the good looking one is August or Gus as he is sometimes called."

Well, come in. Your Aunt's in the kitchen. With everyone gone, we are kind of on our own till spring."

Cherly came in, drying her hands on a kitchen towel. "You're sure you boys aren't twins? Wow, you've got some of your Great Grandma's looks— pretty handsome too. Which one of you is the homely runt?"

"Well, if we look so much alike I guess we both are."

After passing around family news and updates on their cousins, Paul asked them to stay for dinner. Gus then spoke up. "Uncle Paul, we have a proposal for you and your family. Fred and I want to look for the gold mine that Gramps used to finance the first Lazy S ranch."

Fred then spoke up. "Gus graduated from Colorado State, as a mining engineer, and I'm working on a geology degree at Gunnison. You got the ranch, but our dad got the journals and sketchy maps he drew for Great Grandma to look at."

Gus added, "We've talked to various tribes about it, and they can use the money as well. Fred and I combined our middle names, Ouray and Shone, to form The Ouray Shona Mining Company. The site doesn't seem to be on the reservation lands, but it may be on a holy site in the National Forest Lands. We want to set up a trust for the tribes—1/3 for the Ute tribe, 1/3 for the Jenkins family, and 1/3 for the company we have formed.

"That seems pretty straight forward, but what do you want from us? We don't have much available money, and we won't want to start work until spring. Maybe we can work something out," Paul explained.

"We don't need funding now, but may if we find something worthwhile. We just want permission to put a trailer up at the old line camp and have the use of a spare office or a saddle room."

"Well, sure, and you can stop in for a meal and a shower when you show up also," Cherly said. "We'll put your pictures in the office—Ouray and Shona Jenkins, our guest riders. That will surely attract some of the younger women—maybe some of their mothers too."

Gus said, "We would like you to look over the notes and sketches that Great Gramps left. You've been all over this range, so you can clue us in on the topography, and maybe locate some of the land marks mentioned and sketched."

"Sure, I'll dig out some of the government maps and maybe some old range surveys to see if they can help."

"Thanks, Uncle Paul. Fred and I will bring up the trailer and a few horses in the spring. We will keep you in the loop and you can get hold of us through Dad and Mom, if we are out of cellphone range."

With hugs, goodbyes, and good luck ringing in their ears, the Jensen boys drove off into the evening sun glow.

The Family Quarry

The smell of Gold

By Bonnie Bliss

"Damn," Paul thought. "My secret and Sean's will be discovered. Sean and I have been camping in the clearing by the quartz outcropping for years. It is a serene beautiful meadow. Many years back we dug a cave/tunnel into the cliff. What started as a boyhood lark had developed into a comfortable rustic log-cabin. With the secret addition of beds, chairs (each piece brought carefully by horseback up the mountain), and the addition of a fire place, it is now a warm and dry retreat in the backcountry. Sean and I are the only two people who know of its existence."

As a boy, Paul and his cousin, Sean, had spent many summer days along the river, a tributary of the San Luis River. They loved to fly fish and catch trout which could be eaten. They would often camp and eat their fish for dinner—resulting in many happy memories.

The boys were like brothers, growing up together on the remote ranch several miles from town. Their

294

mom's had home schooled the boys, and Sean's mom was also the housekeeper and cook for the main house at the ranch. She also baked fresh cookies for them every afternoon.

Most days after school when their ranch chores were done, the boys would go for a ride, as one of their chores was to exercise the horses. Sean's dad was the farm manager, so he made sure the boys groomed and fed their horses after each ride.

Rosie McDowd, Sean's sister, was the housekeeper now. She had lived on the ranch all of her life. Like Sean, she was the daughter of the Ute branch of the family. She had helped her mother, the old housekeeper, with the bedrooms and in the kitchen. As she learned cooking skills, she took over the kitchen and later became the housekeeper for the ranch. She had played with Paul and Sean when they were young ranch kids.

Sean and his family lived on the ranch in the original homestead cabin that Josh had built for Brighty when they arrived in 1870 as newlyweds. Over the years, of course, the home had been rebuilt and modernized, with more bedrooms added, a modern kitchen installed, and bathrooms updated, too. However the original river rock fireplace was still in place, dominating the living room.

One year when the boys were about 12, there was a drought and the water level in the river dropped to a trickle. They tried to pan for gold using their mess kit plates to scratch the sandy river bottom. They had been lucky that first day and had found a few flakes of gold. After that the river and the gold panning had become addictive. Every chance they could find they went camping along the river, eating fresh trout, and panning for gold. Paul had even found enough in one summer to pay his tuition at college. Of course, by then they were using snorkels and wetsuits in the cold water.

When the boys were teenagers they had ridden their horses up the river into the mountains. On one long weekend they had found the headwaters of the creek that flows through the ranch. Near the top of the valley, it had opened up into a large grassy meadow.

The snow melt was draining from the area by a maze of small streamlets—each a foot or so wide and just a few inches deep—with freezing cold running water. The meadow slope down from a cliff that rose to the mountain peak. The streamlets joined together into a small waterfall leading into the valley below.

The ground was dry up near the cliff so the boys set up their camp there. Using the cliff for protection from the wind, they built their fire pit. The next morning they found they were camped under the quartz outcrop of the family legend.

As Gus and Fred talked, Paul clutched the gold nugget in his pocket. It was the first nugget that he and Sean had found many years ago on one of their fishing trips. In fact, it had certainly prompted them to ride up river into the mountains looking for more gold quartz.

A storm of thoughts kept Paul awake all night. In truth, Paul had at one time seriously considered developing a mine. It was in the third year of a drought, and money was really tight, but he could never allow himself to break the promise he made to his ancestors.

As Gus and Fred told their story, Paul remembered who they were. Paul was descended from five generations of the first born sons from Josh and Brighty. These boys were 3rd or 4th cousins, descended from a younger son of Brighty and Josh.

Judging from their age they were one generation further down the family tree.

Paul's grandfather had a younger brother that had left the ranch in a big huff. He was really angry to be cut out of the ranch inheritance. He left angrily with only the boxes of maps and journals.

Paul's family story was "to cherish and to protect the land's beauty and bounty." The story for these cousins must be that "they got the ranch and we only got a few boxes of old papers. We have been robbed by primogeniture. We deserve our share of the ranch, and we deserve our share of the gold."

As descendants of this younger son/brother their real inheritance was resentment and feelings of persecution. They felt they had been gypped out of their share of the family legacy—the gold bearing quartz mine. Their lives had been spent treading, dreaming, planning, and plotting how to get their share of the promised gold.

Paul could read the greed in their eyes—he could hear it in their voices. But he couldn't believe that the family would choose to ruin their ancestral home. Paul could feel the greed as the boys told of their plans.

They know modern methods of good mining. Were they really willing to desecrate the ranch and the mountain with pit mining, cyanide, mercury, and service roads? Their family dream seemed to be 'One day we will find the gold mine and we will all be rich.'

Paul spent a sleepless night trying to sort out the mining problem. The romantic story was that of gold miners panning for gold in a cold river or creek. That was the story of the 1850's and was gone forever—that kind of gold mine was too inefficient for modern mining.

Mining for gold quartz would certainly desecrate the land. The quartz would have to be mined from the mountain. Then the ground would have to be broken into pieces using stamp mills, and then rinsed through sluice ladders to wash away the dirt and small non-gold bearing mud. All of that work for a few flakes or nuggets of gold.

Desecration of the beautiful mountain was inevitable. The high country Pinion Pine forests would have to be cut, and a saw mill would have to be built to mill the logs into usable timber to support the fine tunnels from collapsing. The forest would die off from the debris of stripping the logs. The disruption of the soil would cause flooding in the valley below. The beautiful fall colors of the Aspen would be lost, also.

Lots of water was a necessity for gold mining. The quartz lies above the meadow at the head waters of the creek. So, placer mining was impossible at that altitude—not enough water. Roads would need to be built to bring the rocks down to the river. That would create big scars on the mountain—and they would lose the forests.

Modern methods of mining involve pit mining and strong chemicals like cyanide, and mercury. Logging roads would need to be built to truck the ore from the mountain to an area to receive the dirt and debris, and the smelters—on and on—forming desecration on all sides.

Paul's nightmares continued. Hard rock miners digging deep tunnels into mountain cliffs, deforested mountains, stamp mills to crush the quartz, and trucks to transport the ore to the smelters. Smoke from the smelters filling the valley. Placer miners, using hydraulic streams of water to erode the dirt to expose the lode bearing rocks—the debris carried downstream, killing the wildlife and plants.

Paul remembered his trip to California, and seeing the miles and miles of gravel and rocks, and the debris left after placer miners stripped the earth of dirt and nutrients. 50 years after the mining, and still not a blade of grass grew on the rubble piles.

When Paul woke up the next day he looked out the windows of his tower bedroom. What a beautiful day it was. And what a beautiful view he had from his tower windows. Before him was his favorite view. Nearly 360 degrees around him he could see his ranch—the home buildings, the stables, the barns, and the riding arenas. He looked down on the Stockman's house, the original house built by Josh for Brighty. Sean still lived there with his oldest son, who was his dad's right hand man in running the cattle business.

Beyond the developed area Paul could see several miles up the valley. Beyond the boundary of the ranch rose the mountains and the treasured quartz mine coveted by his nephews. As he looked upon the land, which was the Jenkins family legacy, he considered his plan of action.

First he would want to find Sean. They could visit the high country camp, maybe even today. They needed to plan to protect the ranch and direct all future development.

Paul knew it was time to check with the BLM about his homestead papers. He needed to verify that the patent was recorded, as that would not allow anyone but him, the owner, to mine for minerals on the land. He leased land from the Forest Service and his US Parks leases would also need to be protected. Having a recorded patent would prevent claim jumpers from developing his land without his consent.

For good measure he would file a lode-mining claim on the quartz outcrop. This would allow him the final word in any development, and would protect the ranch from mining by anyone but the owners. That would protect the area from unauthorized development. He would talk to Sean—together they would form a long term plan for the ranch.

Paul found Sean after breakfast, and by early afternoon their jobs were done and they were heading out. After a quick ride up into the mountains they would be at their cabin before dark.

They had left in such a hurry that they had forgotten to check the weather, so they were surprised when the rain started and turned into snow just before they arrived at the cabin. By the time they fed and bedded the horses, the snow was starting to stick.

Once inside the cabin they lost track of time as they formulated their plans. Both men were surprised the next morning to find they were snowed in. Like all good cowboys, they checked their horses first thing, and then took care of themselves. The horse's lean-to had provided a dry refuge for them—banks of snow kept the wind and wetness outside. The two horses were blanketed and huddled together in a corner, keeping each other warm. Paul pulled down some fresh hay and checked to see that the water trough was not frozen over.

While Paul was checking the horses, Sean was seeing to breakfast. Once the fire was burning again, he heated cans of beans for breakfast. Not a big feast, but just perfect for a snowy morning.

Back at the ranch the families were just waking up. Paul and Sean were discovered to still be gone. In their rush to be away they had failed to tell anyone of their planned trip. Two horses were gone, as well as sleeping bags and food. The Cook reported that the ham-end and bread were missing as well.

Everyone was anxious, but not panicked until the men had been gone a second night. Fortunately or unfortunately, the ranch had experienced several rescues over the years. Several years ago a ranch hand had fallen from his horse and broken his leg. They knew the drill, but this was different—the two most experienced men were now the ones missing.

Cherly called the sheriff and together they organized a search party. The sheriff brought two men with radios, bedding, food, and lights. Soon five men were ready to head out. Harry and Ethel Bromwell, their neighbors, came over to help man the home base.

The rescue party checked on the cattle as they moved up the mountain. They would swing over to the forested part of the mountain, and head further up if needed. They hoped to find Paul and Sean before they had gone that far.

There was now three feet of snow at the ranch house, so further up the mountain there could be four or five feet of snow—probably more than that in drifts. It was still snowing big fat snowflakes, very heavy and wet. These were not the light fluffy flakes that skiers love—the ones that are perfect for deep power skiing. This snow was very heavy and subjected to avalanche.

The men left—loaded down with food, blankets, and camping gear. The women stayed behind to worry and to cook pots of stew, chili, soup, and bread. It was just the kind of food to warm and thaw the cowboys when they returned.

Cherly phoned her children, not to panic them, but to let them know what was happening on the ranch. Harry and Cherly monitored the radio and marked the map charting the search up the mountain.

The cattle were okay. They had been found in a sheltered pasture by some trees. Paul and Sean had been there. They had moved the cattle into the forested area to avoid freezing winds. The water trough was filled and fresh hay was scattered around in the forest, but the men were not there. The cattle were okay for now, but they would need to be moved further down the mountain after the unseasonal storm was past.

After searching the area, the rescuers found signs that the men had headed further up the mountain. What had possessed them to continue up? After radioing headquarters with their findings the rescue party continued up the mountain, too. They camped that night just at the edge of the trees. It was a cold and wet night, but returning home without their friends was unthinkable.

The morning of the third day dawned bright and sunny. The sun on the snow looked like a carpet of diamonds. The trees were loaded down with snow, and the cowboys had to use care when riding under them. If a tree was brushed by a horse, a cold shower of snow would drop down on the cowboy, or worst yet, the branch might break and land on the cowboy, perhaps maiming him or killing his horse.

It is tricky riding in the snow. The danger of avalanche is always present. Cleared areas on a slope often meant past avalanche activity. Better to stay near tree cover, for the snow will be more stable. The search party rode single file higher up the mountain. They stopped for a mid-day lunch break. While the radio report was being sent, they spotted movement on the slope above them.

Could it be Paul and Sean? Yes, it was. They were cutting across a barren area of snow moving toward a line of trees. The rescue party waited anxiously to mark their progress across the new snow, while not moving themselves. What was that old saying? "The third man skiing in virgin snow is a dead man in an avalanche."

When Paul and Sean were safely across the dangerous area, the rescue team made note of their location and waited to be joined by the men. Paul and Sean were embarrassed by all the fuss of the big rescue. They and their horses had been snug and well-fed all night, sheltered inside their well-stocked cabin. The last summer the two men had split and stacked the wood from a downed tree, so they were nice and warm, too.

The good news of the reunion was radioed back to the ranch. Those left behind started cooking a big meal to greet the cold and wet cowboys returning from their adventure. Beds were readied for anyone who wanted to stay over.

Paul and Sean were forced to confess that they had spent the night warm and dry in their secret cabin, but they were very vague about the location of the cabin. No one seemed to notice, as everyone was pleased that the big rescue had a happy ending.

It was time for Paul and Sean to share their secret with their families. The decision to mine or not to mine had long lasting consequences affecting the ranch and the ranch families for generations.

Paul called his children once he was home, fed and warm. They had been worried, and were glad to hear his story. They were open to a trip to Colorado soon. It was time for a family homecoming. He would talk with Cherly and invite all the children home to the ranch this fall. Sean McDowd and his family would be included. They had been farm managers on the ranch for three generations. The ranch was as much theirs as his.

Paul knew the old family story. Out of his respect for the land and his ancestors he had never tried to mine the quartz for gold. Would his strong moral compass allow him to abandon his Great Grandad's promise to the Indians this time?

The Family Quarry

The Conclusion

By Tom Bryant

Paul deliberated long and hard over the issue of revealing the source of the family's gold. He had trouble sleeping. As far as he knew, no one had taken any from the vein since Josh had gathered the original stash to purchase the homestead and the various mineral rights he acquired along the way. The farm had been profitable enough so no extra income had been needed in more than one hundred years. However, he faced a dilemma. His one son Eric had no interest in the ranch or the property. Furthermore, Eric's young son had become citified with no interest in the great outdoors in general or the Colorado ranch in particular.

Paul's daughters were scattered with Lois in Australia and Irene in Italy. Neither one had shown the slightest inclination to return to the US to live on a remote ranch in Colorado. Lois had a couple of young children, but Irene was still footloose and enjoying herself in the Italian opera scene. Besides his own family, Paul worried about the two families that had grown up with the ranch and depended upon the income from its operation—the McDowds and the Bothwells.

What to do with the secret that Great Grandad swore to the Utes? He promised to keep the location secret forever, and he did. He never told a soul. Paul had deduced the location from careful reading of Brighty's notes and a lucky accident. However, with two geologists in the clan, how secure is that? The boys had been panning for gold in the stream that sometimes became a river. The headwaters of that outlet would be one obvious place to look for the mother lode. So there isn't much of a secret any more. Besides, Great-Grandfather has been dead for more than a century. How long is forever?

Paul still feared the spoils from the traditional methods of gold extraction he had seen over the years. Perhaps there are newer, less destructive ways to get the mineral out of the ground. Could he take the secret to his grave? Not likely—if he had found the apostolic mine, so could others. The papers' review with the cousins in Denver taught them that they had considerable control over the mineral deposits, so perhaps lacking an heir with interest in running the ranch the best thing to do is to have a family council and create a company that can manage the assets in a responsible way. They could also sell outright and walk away from any real or perceived obligation to preserve the environment and the commitments to the Utes made so long ago.

First, he needed to have a look at the pit homes once again. They still lay within his boundaries even though the National Park Service staff had declared them prehistoric sites, and therefore off limits to tourists or explorers.

At the end of the week, Paul gathered Gus and Fred for the expedition to the site. Among their gear they carried one of the ranch's radios used to communicate with the cowboys when they were out with the herd. As they approached the area they heard voices. Paul raised his hand for silence and gathered the three of them together. They tethered their horses, a distance away so if they should neigh, the sound would not reach the pit houses.

Paul whispered, "I don't like this. Fred. You take the radio. Get your gun ready and stay hidden, but cover our backs. Make no noise. Keep the radio open

311

and report where we are and tell whoever's on the line with you that there is an intruder in the pit homes. The sheriff should know about that. Gus and I will see what's going on. Okay?" The men nodded.

Fred scuttled further away and started the radio transmission. Paul and Gus moved quietly to a position where they could see the site without being seen. Three men were working in one of the pits. They seemed to be taking material out of one house and loading in into the chest of their ATV.

Paul whispered to Gus, "Get the tag number of that vehicle." Fred appeared at their side and whispered, "Okay, they were glad to know where we are and the sheriff is contacting the Park Service. Between them, they'll send some people up here."

Paul whispered, "That'll take a couple hours. Relay their registration number and then get yourself hidden. Gus and I will have a chat with our visitors."

Allowing Fred time to hide, Paul stood and walked into the clearing where the men were working.

"Oh shit, Carl! We've got company," said one.

One man emerged from the nearest pit house. He walked toward Paul with a swagger and said, "Whacha doing here, cowboy?"

Paul stood his ground and said, "I ask the same of you. This is protected land."

"Who says?"

"National Park service for one, and me for another. I own this property."

Carl snarled. "Look at this here dude claimin' to own the land. Nobody owns Government land. Git away afore I have to make you move." He took out his Colt '44 and waved it menacingly.

"Put that away before somebody gets hurt."

"Hah! Who's gonna make me?"

He rolled the weapon around in his hand, then raised it up and fired it into the air. A second shot followed and Carl collapsed. His gun skittered away as he tried to break his fall.

His buddy rushed to his side. Carl moaned and said, "Joe, Get us the hell out of here."

Joe asked, "Where are you hurt?"

"M'leg. Get the gun."

Paul said, "I'd leave it alone if I were you." He walked to the weapon, wrapped it in his bandana, and

313

picked it up. "I'll take care of it. Don't you worry about that."

He went to Carl's side and examined the wound. "No damage to the artery, but you'd better get going. That leg needs medical attention."

Joe eased Carl onto the ATV and climbed into the driver's seat. The third man came running and jumped onto the storage box behind Carl.

Joe put the ATV in gear and it jerked away.

Paul turned to Gus and said, "I don't think Joe really knows how to drive that thing."

Paul added to Fred who had appeared from his hiding place, "Call the Sheriff to tell him that the intruders are on their way out and need medical attention. I guess they came up the Brokeback trail. That's the only way I know to get a vehicle up here. Meanwhile we'd better see what they did."

Fifteen minutes later, Paul said, "Okay. We see that they've looted three of the five houses. Let's get more brush to cover the entrance to the two they missed and then get ourselves out of here."

As they rode back to the main house, Gus said to Paul, "What are you going to do with the ranch? No one wants the responsibility to run it, yet we know there's gold here somewhere."

"Yes, I know. I've found the place, but I don't have any idea how much is there. We could have found just a few flakes. That was enough to get the ranch started, but there could be lots more."

"You know that between me and Fred we have a good idea for you. You don't need to sell the place. There are companies that would love to operate a lease agreement."

"But they'll leave a big mess."

"Not necessarily. We can write a lease that requires them to restore the land when the gold runs out."

Paul shook his head. "Problem is that there are burials all through the area. The Utes get pretty excited when we mess around with grave sites."

"I know of two outfits that have successfully worked in Indian lands, and when they left, everybody was happy with the outcome. One of these companies is still working their vein. They found a really good one. Why don't I get them out here to give us proposals?"

"We'd need to show them where the gold is."

"True, but as long as you hold the rights, there's nothing anyone can do."

"I don't know about this. Josh promised never to tell."

"For heavens' sake, Paul, you found the source. I'll bet others have found it too. If you're in a region with gold deposits and you know what to look for, these veins are not hard to find."

"I'll think about it." Paul said. "See how Fred is doing. He shot a person and that sometimes is hard on a guy. The hospital just called and the guy he shot is going to be okay. Turns out he was one of the commission members who were supposedly protecting the pit-homes from looters. He's got bigger problems than a flesh wound."

Four months later, Paul gathered the clan in the main room of the ranch house. He had everyone there that could be. Eric had come from New England. Paul had arranged telephone connections open to Lois in Australia and to Irene in Italy. Gus and Fred were the main attractions.

Fred began, "We've done a detailed analysis of this deposit and I can assure you that it's not the Mother Lode. There are many tiny deposits throughout this region of the Great Basin and by this time all the good ones have been found and exploited."

"You mean there's not much there anymore?" said Lois.

"No, there never was much in that vein. What's more, it's pretty low grade. There's lots of copper mixed in with the gold, so the yield is not great. Your Great-Grandfather got a very good deal when he sold his gold, because the assay methods were primitive. After the second assay, no one bothered him for details of where he had found it because it wasn't very good."

Eric said, "Well, can't we get a company to mine it anyway? There is gold in the rock. Surely with the price of gold today, that's got to be worth something."

Fred said, "True. It's worth something, but the cost of extraction is also quite high. With today's market conditions, the gold in that ore will not cover the cost of separating it out on a small scale. The deposit doesn't appear to be big enough to justify a large investment and what's more, the Utes would never agree to that with the number of burial sites in these mountains."

317

Irene said, "So Great-Grandpa's gold mine is a fraud and we can't expect a fortune. What a disappointment."

Fred said, "I hope none of you has mortgaged your home on the expectation. There's nothing there."

Eric said, "That's bad news. I had counted on a bit of a boost from Great-Grandpa."

Paul spoke, "As a result, of this, I think we can forget about Great-Grandpa's gold and focus on our own destinies. Since no one wants to take over, I propose to sell the place. I've had several good offers for the stable business even without the dressage school. The range part is also attractive, so even without the gold mine we've got a valuable property that will fetch a good price. My plan is to sell out and keep half of the proceeds for myself and split the other half in thirds. Eric, you may find yourself out of the hole after all and without having to wait for me to die."

"What will you do, Dad?" Irene said.

"I'm tired of ranching, so I'll move to town and spend my time traveling around. I saw a bit of the world while I was in college, but I'd like to see more.

So, unless there are more questions that I can't answer, this meeting is adjourned."

No one spoke, so the telephones reverted to dial tone and the family dispersed.